DREAD JOURNEY

DOROTHY B. HUGHES (1904–1993) was a mystery author and literary critic. Born in Kansas City, she studied at Columbia University and published her mystery debut, *The So Blue Marble*, in 1940.

Hughes published fourteen more novels, three of which were made into successful films (*In a Lonely Place*, *The Fallen Sparrow*, and *Ride the Pink Horse*). In the early fifties, Hughes largely stopped writing fiction, preferring to focus on criticism, for which she would go on to win an Edgar Award. In 1978, the Mystery Writers of America presented Hughes with the Grand Master Award for lifetime achievement. *Dread Journey* is her eighth novel.

SARAH WEINMAN is the author of *The Real Lolita: The Kidnapping of Sally Horner and the Novel That Scandalized the World*. She also edited the anthologies *Women Crime Writers: Eight Suspense Novels of the 1940s & '50s* and *Troubled Daughters, Twisted Wives*, and writes the "Crime Lady" column at CrimeReads, where she is a contributing editor. She lives in Brooklyn, New York.

DREAD JOURNEY

DOROTHY B. HUGHES

Introduction by
SARAH WEINMAN

**AMERICAN
MYSTERY
CLASSICS**

*Penzler Publishers
New York*

For Rose

Published in 2019 by Penzler Publishers
58 Warren Street, New York, NY 10007
penzlerpublishers.com

Distributed by W. W. Norton.

Cover image: Andy Ross
Cover design: Mauricio Diaz

Paperback ISBN 9781613161463
Hardcover ISBN 9781613161456
eBook ISBN 9781480426955

Library of Congress Control Number: 2019906556

Printed in the United States of America.

9 8 7 6 5 4 3 2 1

DREAD JOURNEY

INTRODUCTION

"Dorothy B. Hughes (1904–1993)—the B stands for Belle, and Hughes replaced her maiden name, Flanagan, when she married Lewis Hughes in 1932—is my favorite crime writer. Full stop." I wrote these sentences in 2012, for an essay published by the *Los Angeles Review of Books,* and now, nearing the end of 2019, I have not altered my opinion in the slightest.

The steadfastness of that opinion owes largely to my love of Hughes' 1947 novel *In a Lonely Place,* which I've reread every year since 2004. That first read remains an indelible memory, because it coincided with my gradual leap from passionate crime fiction fan to professional writer. (The good thing about earning a living as a writer, however, is that it doesn't detract from being a fan of the best stuff.)

Hughes' post-World War II novel, which had then been reissued by The Feminist Press and more recently republished by NYRB Classics, blasted my tender young mind open to new ways of reading. I marveled at Hughes's ability to let readers in on what was *really* happening under the nose of her thoroughly unreliable narrator, Dix Steele, while he remained in the dark about his own nefarious motivations and about the women who would see to his undoing and seal his fate. Hughes, more than seven decades ago, depicted the psyche and actions of a serial killer with such psychological accuracy that FBI profilers would learn a few things from immersing themselves in her prose.

In the decade and a half since my first encounter with *In a Lonely Place* (also the source material for the fine, but very different, film starring Humphrey Bogart and Gloria Grahame) I've made my way through the entirety of Hughes's crime fiction *oeuvre*, including that formidable stretch of eleven novels published between her first, *The So Blue Marble* (1940), reissued last year by Penzler Publishers, and *In a Lonely Place*.

Hughes was that rare bird who couldn't write a turkey. She built worlds—especially in the early New York novels and the later ones set around Los Angeles' twisting streets and in New Mexico's wide-open spaces—that were vivid with bright colors, glittering baubles, and big dreams, yet never felt cartoonish. Her main characters stood outside ruling classes and governments, took part in clandestine operations trying to unseat evil, and overcame damaged pasts and terror-filled presents with resilience and toughness that surprised even them. Hughes, in other words, plumbed three-dimensional depths, no matter the plot device or twist.

Ride The Pink Horse (1946) and *The Expendable* Man (1963) are often cited as Hughes' other masterpieces, and I concur. The most welcome surprise for me, though, was *Dread Journey*, published two years prior to *Lonely Place;* the novel hardly merited much critical coverage in 1945, and largely fell off the crime fiction map—until now.

Dread Journey, as told by a different writer, would be a more conventional locked-room mystery: a cast of characters in various states of psychological distress all sharing space on the same Pullman luxury train traveling across the country. Someone dies, and the death, initially written off as a drug overdose, is later realized as a murder, with a handful of likely suspects who carried—or were perceived to carry—a grudge. There might even be a detective already on the train, or about to hop on, to solve the mystery. That detective might be Hercule Poirot, and this novel might be *Murder on the Orient Express*.

Dorothy B. Hughes, however, wasn't writing a locked-room mystery, but a suspense novel steeply suffused with the dread of the novel's title. The premise, more than a little prosaic, traps all of the novel's characters on a cross-country train from Los Angeles to New York and inevitably destines one of them for death far short of the train's final destination. But we don't know when and we don't know who, not at the outset. What is more important, to her and then to the reader, are the studies she makes of her characters, almost all of whom have some tie to Hollywood, and almost all of whom begin as tropes, but deepen into far more interesting figures.

These characters include the big star about to fall (Kitten Agnew), the producer/director yearning to destroy her (Vivien Spender) and the producer's loyal, long-suffering assistant (Mike Dana), the star's malleable, about-to-ripen replacement (Gratia Shawn), a playboy bandleader on the periphery (Leslie Augustin), and the desperate, failed screenwriter skulking back home to mama (Sidney Pringle). Removed from Hollywood are two other men: the porter, James Cobbett, who sees everything but is left alone and underestimated because of class (service) and race (black), and Hank Cavanaugh, the once-hotshot reporter who has descended into alcoholism after seeing too much at the front. Uniting almost all of the cast members, in direct and indirect ways, is a dream, as personified by the role of Clavdia Chaucat, a Cleopatra-like literary figure rich in complexity.

For Kitten, Clavdia personifies her burgeoning ambition as a serious actress to transcend Spender's clutches. For Viv, the part of Clavdia is his ultimate chance to turn fantasy into reality, the part dangled to woman after woman who did not meet his Galatea-like ideal; when they fail, he sets out to destroy them. For Gratia, it's an opportunity, the enormity of the stakes remaining just out of reach. And for the other men in their orbit—Les, Hank, and Sidney—Clavdia is a conduit for their own thwarted dreams, disappointments, and redemption quests.

Gratia in particular is a classic Hughes character, one presented through the lens of others—especially men, another classic Hughes gambit—while the reader suspects something else is going on underneath the surface. Kitten senses this depth, even voices it at times, but the most astute comment emerges from Hank: "Gratia could look out for herself; however unworldly she appeared, that very quality was her protection. It was Kitten with all her brazen world wisdom who was helpless."

Viv Spender may be Hughes' most overt villain, even more so than the psychopathic twins who charm and scheme and manipulate their way through *The So Blue Marble*. Spender is a man with an indomitable God complex, ready to crush anyone in his way ("He's as sane as you or I," Les Augustin tells Gratia Shawn late in *Dread Journey*, "With one small exception. He thinks he's Almighty God"). But even overt villains have understandable motivations. "One thing that money and power and importance did to a man. It made him lone," Cobbett notices with particular clarity. But Spender's unhealthy obsessions are best understood through his secretary who has witnessed her boss at his worst, and still remained with him.

Mike, like Kitten and like Gratia, is a product of internalized misogyny. She knows all of Spender's dark secrets but remains with him out of loyalty and out of some deeper connection she can only admit to herself, even as it's patently obvious to others (one suspects that James Cobbett, the all-observing, all-analyzing porter, sussed this out immediately, even as he wouldn't venture to express this opinion to anyone else). So it's especially satisfying that Mike gets the crime fiction equivalent of an eleven o'clock number, where the depths of her feelings, her own sublimated rage and desire for justice, are all aired—it's a star turn that is well worth the wait, and earns its catharsis.

Hughes' choice of omniscient viewpoint invites the reader into the characters' inner sancta and excavates their fears, their desires, their jealousies, their dreams with the most exacting literary scalpel. There is triumph, but the aftertaste was never more bitter and pungent.

Every sentence of *Dread Journey* carries the weight of the tragic events that will unfold over the course of the novel. But Hughes has also written a sly portrait of how Hollywood worked then and, as the #MeToo movement that erupted in earnest in the fall of 2017 showed, still works now: insecure, powerful men lusting for greater power, innocents thrust into situations beyond their control, and terrible contracts besting everybody.

Dread Journey was published a year after Dorothy B. Hughes moved to Los Angeles. She had published seven novels and one, *The Fallen Sparrow*, had already been adapted into a 1943 film starring John Garfield and directed by Richard Wallace. (Films of *Ride The Pink Horse* and *In A Lonely Place* followed in 1947 and 1950, respectively.) This was boom time for suspense stories, and women writers like Hughes, Vera Caspary, Marty Holland, and Gertrude Walker found ample work writing scripts, adaptations of their own novels or original treatments.

But *Dread Journey* never made it to the screen. I wonder why, but I also do not. The observations about Hollywood are too pointed, even for an industry already pretending to be interested in self-reflection (*A Star Is Born*, the original version, was less than a decade in the past). Women may have been paid, even well, but never on par with their male counterparts. Hughes had a family to support. Less than a decade later, she would put

vi · SARAH WEINMAN

family over work, going on a novel-writing hiatus between *The Davidian Report* (1952) and *The Expendable Man* (1963). And after that latter novel, there would be none more.

Interviews with Hughes often asked after favorites of her own novels. She made, to my mind, curious judgments, mostly by not mentioning *In a Lonely Place*. Was it, and *Dread Journey*, mere hackwork to Hughes? She never said, and we'll never know. The work can transcend the writer, and Dorothy B. Hughes had so much talent, and so much precision, that masterpieces emerged out of the constraints of genre.

Dread Journey is a prime example of this transcendence. The novel, with this choice reissue, should take its rightful place among the upper echelon of Hughes' body of work, and of twentieth century crime fiction as a whole.

—SARAH WEINMAN

ONE

"I'M AFRAID."

She had spoken aloud. She hadn't meant to; she hadn't wanted those words to come up from her throat to her lips. She hadn't meant to think them, much less speak them. She didn't want Gratia to have heard them.

But across the room the girl lifted her eyes from her book.

"What did you say?" she queried.

—2—

James Cobbett rested on the small leather seat at the end of the aisle. He could rest; this was the mid-afternoon lull. A little later the bells would start buzzing again, for drinks at that time. The routine never varied. This was the great Chief. Stow them in at noon, bells buzzing until they'd jogged down into their cubicles. After that the lunch exodus, and bells for those who shunned the public diner. Big shots or those who thought they were, those trying to be. So big they couldn't be seen in public although they budgeted gargantuan amounts yearly to be kept in the eye of the public. After lunch, bells for little nervous things, and then the settling down was complete, then the lull and

James Cobbett could rest. When the cocktail bells started, there wouldn't be any rest until late. The Chief didn't go to bed early. Cobbett would make up the beds according to routine, and if permitted, but there would be some who would cajole or bribe. It would be past midnight before this night's work would be ended.

Sometimes James Cobbett read during the lulls, sometimes he just sat there swaying with the train, looking out at the scenery so familiar as to pass unseen. Sometimes he thought long thoughts. He wasn't thinking them now. He was cataloguing the animals occupying his cages on this run. They weren't unusual; they were of such a sameness he could have prophesied what each one was doing behind his closed door and just what he would do from here to Chicago. In the house of economics he could tell just what to expect of each one at the end of the journey. It must be the monotony that made him feel as he did, depressed, almost morose. He didn't often feel lowdown, he was of nature cheerful; maybe he was catching cold at the mere thought of Chicago's snow. Meantime there was nothing out of the ordinary in his passengers, the usual Chief passengers. The same run, the same kind of people.

Vivien Spender, the great Viv Spender, was in drawing room A. He wouldn't be any trouble; he was too important a Hollywood name for that, but he'd expect plenty of service. He would pay for it. He could afford to; he was one of the six high names in the Treasury Department list. His salary was publicized yearly at well over the half-million mark. Salary that was; there wasn't any information given on what he made above that from bonuses and dividends and royalties. The kind of big money that came to those who had big money. James Cobbett didn't believe any man was worth a salary of a half-million dollars a year. What could a man do with that much money? After you had a house and furnishings and all the cars you wanted, maybe a ranch because you felt secure in land; clothes, food—put all essentials and luxuries together and you didn't make a dent on the half million. Not when you were receiving it every year. Viv Spender had been getting it for a dozen years and more. James Cobbett wondered what that much money would do for a man, for the inside man.

This was the first time Viv Spender had been on the Chief. Spender traveled by plane. This time he'd changed his habits. Maybe he wasn't in any hurry. Maybe he'd acquired air nerves. A lot of men did after a while. For a man of importance, Spender on face value was a real enough person. He was big physically, as tall as James Cobbett, broader of shoulder, heavier of hip. He admitted to forty-five years; he looked younger. He had a thatch of straw-colored hair, no gray in it, a bit of curl as if he'd plastered it but it wouldn't stay plastered. He had a hearty voice, a quick smile that went from his mouth to the corners of his eyes. His clothes were good. James Cobbett admired good material, rough imported tweeds, handmade boots of the best russet leather. Cobbett didn't covet them; he admired, knowing they were not for him, none the less appreciative of their touch.

Drawing room B was the girls. If they had friends on board, they wouldn't be troublesome. If they were looking for friends and found them, they might be a little noisy but not troublesome. If neither happened, they'd keep the buzzer going tomorrow from sheer boredom. There were two of them. One was strictly Hollywood, gold hair below her shoulders, touched-up, dark eyelashes to make her eyes look larger, a big sulky mouth redder than raw meat. She must be someone, her gray tailored suit was expensive, her narrow black alligator pumps were tall heeled, her stockings sheer as cobwebs. She had the typical Hollywood figure forced into the plain lines of the suit but not hiding the protuberances Hollywood affected. She was as artificial as a doll.

The other girl wasn't so easy to put in a frame. Maybe a paid companion. A dark wool dress, one strand of pearls not real, dark hair. He hadn't had a real look at her yet, the other one had done all the ordering around. The other one was accustomed to spotlight, she took it even in a Pullman drawing room.

The compartments were about the same as always. The one next drawing room A had the young couple, honeymooners. A sweet-faced girl who looked as if she belonged in her suit, proud of the new gold band on her finger. The young husband was clean and eager and a little embarrassed. Not as sure of himself as the girl, women were better pretenders. All the relatives had been hopping around like birds when the couple got on at Pasadena. Debby and Fred Crandall—the names had been carolled in farewell—would be no trouble on this run. Fred had to be back at the office Monday, a short honeymoon. They'd want only to be left alone. And he could make up their berth early. Cobbett smiled. He and Mary had had a weekend honeymoon. He'd rented a car and they'd driven up to the Dells. Six years ago. He hoped the Crandalls in six years would be as happy as the Cobbetts. Maybe not; they were used to more. If you weren't used to happiness, you coddled it, coaxed it into little blooms. You hoarded what you could lay your heart on, to warm you from the great unhappiness of an alien world.

The poet was in the next compartment. He looked like a poet, he was fair and fragile, but as a matter of fact he was Leslie Augustin; there'd been a wire for him as the train left. James Cobbett knew that name. Leslie Augustin was the hottest white band leader in the business. On the air he had a soft speaking drawl, but he sang a sizzling bass. He looked like a poet; instead of misty words, he wrote stomps and jamborees and hoedowns. He didn't look well; even the tan of his face didn't give him a look of health.

The fellow Augustin had brought back with him after lunch was long and lanky and drunk. Not troublesome drunk, but vague-eyed and stiff-gaited. Drunk at two o'clock in the afternoon. He was wearing a hat and a necktie so he couldn't have been in California long.

Next was the old couple, heading back home after a winter in California. They had money; the man might have been a big boss once, now he was gray and shrunken in his clothes. The, woman was small and neat and, like little Joe, wore blue-white diamond rings. They'd been courteous rather than querulous getting settled; they wouldn't bother anyone beyond maybe a request for an extra blanket or pillow. He didn't have to worry about them.

In the compartment next to drawing room B was the solitary man. James Cobbett knew him without knowing him. A man venting his anger at himself on men like himself who had bettered themselves. Having no reason but anger, and out of anger the impulse to destroy. This one looked like a writer, heading back East out of failure. His fear was covered well by the bitterness on him and his anger, but beneath them was fear. He wouldn't demand much; he would be ashamed because he could offer only a niggardly tip. If possible, he would slip off the train at Chicago without any payment for services. Plenty traveled the Chief who hadn't the money for a shoe shine. It was in their contract: first class transportation back to despair.

The usual people of the Chief, good and bad, mixed up, none of them quite the same as they'd be if they were at home, not isolated in rushing space. James Cobbett sat swaying beneath the dignity of the framed sign which stated:

This car is served by

James Cobbett, Porter

And the Chief roared on into the great American desert.

—3—

She was afraid. It wasn't a tremble of fear. It was a dark hood hanging over her head. She was meant to die. That was why she was on the Chief speeding eastward. This was her bier.

If only Gratia weren't so beautiful. Beauty was catnip to him. What was in her face that was a melody even another woman, a woman who hated her, could hear? Katherina Agnew, the famous Kitten Agnew, looked across the compartment at the face bent over the small green-backed book. Take it apart and what was there? A squarish shape over the strong bones, dark hair brushed away from a forehead, only the faintest touch of curl. Not glamorous, just a plain soft sheath of dark hair curved below the ears. Eyes wide, gray, dark-lashed. A small straight nose, yes. A sweet mouth, not too red. The square cleft chin. When you put it together why was it so beautiful?

By all screen standards Kitten's face had it all over this one. Hers was piquant—she knew by rote all the adjectives with which it had been described—the face of a lovely child. Her eyes were amber brown, round and long lashed, they could smolder or fleck joy with equal ease according to what the man of the moment desired. Her mouth was full and rich; her nose, thanks to modern science, as good as Gratia Shawn's. Her hair, honey-colored, rippled to her shoulders. Her figure had all the provocation that Gratia's straight, slim, narrow-shouldered one lacked. Yet he had seen Gratia and even Kitten knew he meant to have Gratia. She knew bitterly that Gratia had a beauty on which no one could put a finger. None the less it was there, serene, changeless and shining.

She didn't have to die. She could go to him now and release him of all obligation. He would in turn release her from the verdict of death. She knew he meant to kill her. It was the only way he could be rid of her unless she released him. She had too much on him for him to discard her as he had discarded all of her predecessors.

When she became Viv Spender's newest discovery, Kitten had knowledge of her predecessors, of their brief candles, of the snuffings out. The one in a home for alcoholics. The one picked up soliciting. The one who jumped from a window while Viv was in Florida with the new. And the others, returned to the drabness from which they had once hopefully emerged, walled behind counters, playing walk-ons. Before he discovered Kitten, when she knew he was about to discover her, she had arranged that she would not be snuffed out. Her lawyer was one of the most respected in law, feared and admired in the colony. From the very beginning he had known each step of her progress. He was ready to sue, ready to break Viv Spender. Not for money alone; because one of the tragic brief candles had been his niece.

Viv Spender could supplant Kitten Agnew, could offer the part of Clavdia to another, but he would be broken if he did. There would be a prison sentence to face. He was too powerful to face it. He had become so powerful that his pride was one with himself.

So powerful he would mete out death? She didn't believe it. She couldn't believe it. Mike hadn't meant that.

Mike had been sent by him to make Kitten cancel this trip. She understood Mike's purpose in trying to frighten her. If she'd worn a black veil and held a roiled crystal, Mike might have frightened her. But it was only Mike, the pearl-above-price private secretary to Viv Spender. The secretary every producer in Hollywood had tried unsuccessfully to steal away. Mike, homely in a land where beauty was the commonplace, unemotional where emotion was the norm, stable where stability was suspicious.

Mike had put on a good act. Sliding in that implication as if it were her own idea. Everyone knew that Mike didn't act without his direction; there was no Mike except in co-existence with him. Mike had not frightened her, only angered her and set her determination. Kitten hadn't known about Gratia then. She hadn't even known yesterday when the publicity department begged her to take the unknown under her wing on this New York safari. It had seemed rather odd to be asked to share her drawing room, but it had been put up to Kitten in such a way that she couldn't refuse. Her publicity was built on the legend of a natural, normal girl, with a great loving heart. Human, good fellow, sympathetic. They'd told her about her invitation—after they'd sent out the publicity. *Kitten Agnew invites a bit girl to share her drawing room.* There was nothing to do but go along with it. He had planned it that way, to goad her, to penalize her even in this petty manner.

She hadn't known until half an hour ago that this girl was the one who was to take her place. He'd kept it that secret no one had known but he himself. Possibly Mike Dana. He had no secrets from Mike; he might think he had but he hadn't. The girl, Gratia Shawn herself, didn't know. And Kitten wouldn't have known but for a casual question, put out of early boredom with the long journey, they were only now entering the desert; out of curiosity about this girl who sat quietly in the chair reading a small green-backed book.

She had asked, "What are you reading?"

Gratia had lifted her eyes, her shining eyes. She'd been too deeply immersed actually to hear Kitten's question. "It's wonderful. Mr. Spender asked me to read it." Her smile was innocent as a white flower. "To see if I liked the part."

It was then that Kitten actually saw the book. An out-of-print edition, from his own bed table. A book she'd held but never read. It was too long to read, too many big thoughts. She forced her suspicions into a seemingly idle question. "What's the part?"

"Clavdia Chauchat."

She didn't hear what else Gratia had to say. Because that was her part. For four years she'd waited for it, been promised it. And because she was shrewd and had struck when she was catnip, she had an unbreakable contract for the role. He'd been promising to produce the picture for years; it was his obsession and his dream. He had discovered innumerable Clavdias but because Kitten was just a little shrewder than he, because she was still closer to her meager beginnings, she or no one would play the part. She had refused to sell him the contract at the time of their most bitter quarrel, four months ago. She had offered to trade it to him for marriage. He might have killed her then if they hadn't been in his office. But she hadn't been afraid of him, of the names with which he'd slapped her face. Everything was in her hands. She hadn't known about the first Mrs. Spender then.

She didn't have to die. She could go to him now, tell him in Gratia Shawn he'd found the perfect Clavdia Chauchat. She could bow out still playing the publicity department's role of the good sport, Kitten Agnew. A part wasn't more important than her life. Failure to attain the star she'd fixed, to be Mrs. Vivien Spender, wasn't as humiliating as death. The fixed star of being Mrs. Spender had risen when he first discovered in Kitten the perfect Clavdia. She knew he'd marry Clavdia Chauchat. He'd been obsessed by the dream for too long.

She could give up everything. She wouldn't have to return to the depressing poverty from which she'd emerged. She'd come a long way from North Dakota before she ever met Viv Spender. The chorus, modeling, band singing. In four years he'd made her a glistening Hollywood star. If she left him, she could go at once to any other lot. She wouldn't be like the others, dropping into oblivion or worse because he'd dismissed her. She didn't love him; she'd never loved him, mad as she'd been about him those first years. He'd been her opportunity. She wasn't like the others, the mechanical doll into which he alone could breathe life. She could stand on her own feet, go on to bigger contracts, more important roles even than Clavdia Chauchat.

But she remembered Rosaleen who had been a great star for the brief interlude; and Titania, where was she? Without his life breath, they had become ghosts. She was afraid.

He wouldn't kill her. It was absurd to consider such a thing. He wouldn't dare. He had too much self-love to risk the fond self against execution. He'd know he couldn't get away with murder.

He would realize it was better to pay, to allow her to be Clavdia—she'd be magnificent in the role. Or to marry; the marriage would be million-dollar publicity, and he could be free after he settled some of those millions on her. She had no intention of letting him frighten her into giving him his cold-blooded way. She'd almost frightened. That weakness was over and done with.

He wouldn't risk killing her. Not unless he could get away with it . . . It was then she whispered to herself but aloud, "I'm afraid."

And the lovely Gratia, not hearing words but only knowing they had been spoken, looked up and asked, "What did you say?"

—4—

Cavanaugh said, "I like it here. I'll stay." His voice didn't sound drunk. It was loud and firm. Maybe it was too loud but he didn't give a damn. Anyone who didn't like it could get the hell out. He stretched himself out across the seats, closed his eyes.

He kept them closed only for a moment. When he shut out sight, he knew he was drunk. It was too early in the clay to pass out. It was a waste of good booze to pass out now. He'd be awake again by midnight. Awake and sober. Awake and agonizing. He shook his head and groaned, "Don't do that."

"Don't do what?" The voice was vaguely amused.

The swirling hammers quieted. He focused his eyes on the man in the seat across. He scowled, "I know who you are. Leslie Augustin." His tongue was thick on the Leslie and he sampled it again with odd pleasure.

"And this is my compartment." The slight voice was still amused.

"Yeah. And how a guy like you rates a compartment and all I got is a lousy upper is what makes proletariats out of honest bourgeoisie."

"I'm the great Augustin," Augustin said pleasantly.

"Yeah? You got a compartment. I got an upper. Can't do any honest drinking in an upper. The fat dame below says the guggle-guggle keeps her awake. I'll stay."

"You'll sleep in the upper if you do," Augustin smiled. "It's my compartment."

Cavanaugh yawned. "You're selfish, Augustin. You Goddamn, lousy, selfish prostitute, you."

Leslie Augustin yawned back at him. "It's my compartment."

Hank Cavanaugh looked out the window. He'd grabbed the window side. The landscape was going too fast and it was jiggling. He shuddered. "Ugh." The landscape was too much like other landscape, barren wasteland. He was thankful his eyes were bleared. He turned them again on Leslie Augustin. Yeah, it was the same Augustin, still looking undernourished though he was undernourished now in a handwoven dust-colored lounging suit, not shiny serge pants. The fair-haired Augustin, an élégant today, the patina of success gold-dusted all over him. Once he'd been skinny, now he was slender; once he'd been unwashed, now he was immaculate; the broken nails had mended, they tapered in a discreet manicure. He still looked like a tall young angel, but his narrow cobalt eyes weren't vengeful as once, they were merely cynical.

"How'd you do it?" Hank Cavanaugh demanded.

"How did I do what?" Leslie lifted a bored cigarette to his thin mouth. He shouldn't be smoking; he had a cigarette cough that would kill a horse.

"What? What do you think? Last time I saw you, you were a stinking poor fiddler—"

Leslie interrupted mildly, "I wasn't a poor fiddler. I was a magnificent fiddler."

"I suppose you can tell me you weren't poor when I fed you out of my own plate weeks on end."

"Yes, I was poor but not a poor fiddler." The thin mouth thinned then curved. "I was poor. And I'd rather be a rich prostitute."

"How'd you do it?" Hank started to shake his head, remembered in time to hold it rigid. "How?"

"I realized," and this time Leslie Augustin didn't bother to put the curve in his mouth, "I wasn't a Menuhin or a Heifetz. Nor a Beethoven nor Tchaikovsky. I'd better give the public what it wanted." He moved his beautiful tapered fingers. "I wrote a stomp."

"A what?"

"A stomp—"

"How d'ya spell it?"

Leslie stomped one foot languidly on the Pullman carpet. "Like that. Stomp." He raised his fleet eyebrows. "My God, Hank, don't tell me you've never heard of the Augustin stomp? Where have you been the last years?"

"Away." The monosyllable was grim. It stopped foolish questioning. But he'd forgotten that Leslie resembled the fairy prince only in appearance. Beneath that beautiful head was a tight, shrewd nugget of a brain, lively as a monkey's, insatiable for factual crumbs about his fellows, crumbs that kneaded together might turn into tasty pattycake for one Augustin. Hank Cavanaugh had despised the fiddler even when he kept him from starvation in New York. Leslie had been a crumb picker then. Plenty of yarns Hank had run down following the crumb trail.

Leslie said with mock humility, "I caught on. A good publicity man, the radio, platters, personal appearances . . . The war helped."

Hank spoke in choked anger, "What about the war?"

Leslie's eyes opened on him. "I've played the U.S.O. circuit."

"Carrion."

Leslie said appeasingly, "I'm sorry, Hank. It's all I've been able to do. I have scars on both lungs."

"Camille in fancy pants."

Leslie flushed slowly. It went away leaving the tan of his cheeks pale. "It's true. The doctors want me to go to Arizona for a long rest. But I won't quit now. I won't quit until I have . . . enough."

"For diamond-studded caviar three times a day."

Leslie smiled a little. "Maybe that's it. I won't stop until I'm sure I'll never go back to a hall bedroom. And cadging meals." The smile was like a knife. "The doctors say if I'd lived right I'd have skipped it. I should have stuck to plenty of fresh milk and green vegetables and twelve hours sleep a night when I was young." The smile was deliberately amused. "For God's sake, don't tell Viv Spender. He'll try to type cast me as Hans Castorp."

"Who the hell is Viv Spender?"

Leslie coughed in amusement. "For God's sake, don't talk so loud! He's in this car. Who is Viv Spender? Vivien Spender? The Gaekwar of Culver City! The Hearst of New Essany! The Zeus of America's greatest industry!" His voice was good natured. "He's a moving-picture producer."

"You in the movies too?" Hank growled.

Leslie shook his head. "I've done a few. Not for Spender. For him I'm holding out for a million-dollar contract." He took from his pocket a gold cigarette case. It was too long and too slender, thin as a ribbon, but the cigarette he took from it was uncrushed. There was engraving inside the cover.

Hank held out his hand. Leslie passed the case, "Sorry." Deliberately Hank split it open, read the enscrolled message. "For the great Augustin with love, Valerie Van Houten." He clipped the case together, said dryly, "Whew."

"She wants to marry me."

"Why not? There's gold in them thar oil."

"I'm not that kind of a prostitute." Leslie replaced it in his pocket. His eye was shrewd, but not malicious. "What have you done for the war?"

Hank closed his eyes. He blanked memory but his tongue was vicious. "I've played carrion. Like you. I've wept crocodile tears on paper for suffering humanity. I've swilled while they starved." He broke off. He'd realized. He wasn't seeing pinwheels. He said, "I'm getting sober. Let's have a drink."

—5—

It had been years since she'd remembered Althea. Because he had forgotten, she had forgotten. Her life was that completely integrated with his.

She had known the first time she saw him that this was as it would be. Perhaps in that first meeting, she had dreamed it was to be the same with him. You are my life, and, you are my life. She had been young then, and the young dared dream even in the immutable face of realities. The young dared expect storybook perfection.

When she met him she still had faith in the old legends. Love would transform the ugly duckling into the exquisite swan. Beauty was not in the mask of a face, it was in the mind and the spirit and the grace beneath the mask. The legends were not without basic truth. Other men had cared for her. She could have married time over, married into love. But her love was given. And for him beauty was the beauty of flesh. Only by this beauty were his senses stirred.

She had learned him quickly; he wasn't hard to fathom in those early years. He was too young, too intense to play a part. Of necessity he learned later to perform. When he learned he performed magnificently; everything he did was magnificent.

In those early years, she could have severed the cord that bound her to him. There would have been some bleeding, a resultant scar, but she would have had freedom. She deliberately chose to be a part of him. Deliberately, if there was deliberate choice. Perhaps a trace of the dream remained, would always remain. At any rate she chose him and her serfdom.

She had never regretted. She had long ago accepted the fact that he would never love her. However, love, or what passed for love with him, the madness which afflicted him in cycles, was a minor part of him. The major portion was hers; the drive to greatness, the brilliance of his creations, the artistic integrity which consumed him, and whose flames blazed his path to glorious success. He was a great artist, an inspired artist. And she was the woman of his artistic life. By giving herself, by offering herself to be possessed by him, she alone possessed him. The legends thus were true. He was hers, all of him, save his love. The minute quality of love.

Althea had hurt. It was because she was still young then, still dreaming. Then came Althea.

He met Althea at a party. He'd gone up a bit in pictures by then, he was mentioned as promising. It was beyond the days when his clothes were shabby when he was careful to keep his feet on the floor during an interview for a job lest the holes in his shoes be seen. By then he had a little car and a small apartment. Mike used to go over on Sundays and clean it. Sometimes she'd wash out his socks. There'd been girls during those first years;

she'd find traces of them, lipstick on a towel, a forgotten hand-kerchief. They hadn't hurt. They were girls the way any young man had girls; pretty, shallow, a momentary diversion.

It wasn't that way with Althea. She had beauty, a strange, flower-like sort of beauty. The fragility of a spray of blossoms, of a slant of sunlight or the shimmering mist after spring rain. Mike wasn't jealous of her, not after she knew her. Althea was real. She was in love with Viv, and if he ever loved, his love was given to her.

If Mike's heart split it was in the darkness of solitude and no one knew. He never knew. She put it together neatly with friendship. She and Viv went on as before. Only she didn't go to his apartment on Sundays to clean; Althea kept the apartment shining and polished. Surprisingly, she became Althea's friend. There was no jealousy in either; between women who loved the same man there was an honest friendship. After Althea, Mike never had another woman for friend.

His star rose quickly in those years. If she didn't see as much of them after they moved to a new and beautiful home, and to a more beautiful and larger home, it was because with success came not only a greater pressure of work, but of social necessity. Beneath it the bond was unbroken.

She didn't know when he was done with Althea. To this day, she didn't know. There was a succession of women moving through his life. That was his business, a procurer of women. For the pleasure of the millions whose drug was the moving pic-tures. Women whose stock in trade was the quivering of a man's nerves, women ripe as sweet figs, lush as pomegranates.

Which one was first, she didn't know. Until his sins were fla-grant, she didn't know. Even then, like Althea, she clung to belief that this was aberration, not the man.

When Althea died, Mike believed that Viv was saved. She

was there that morning, called by him; she witnessed his tempestuous grief. It was she who raised his head from Althea's motionless breast, who led him away to weep on her own unloved breast. In that moment there was dark shameful triumph in her which even her own regret for Althea could not overcome. She believed he would be done with love now, that all his energy would be given his work.

She didn't really know Viv Spender until after Althea died. She learned him down the succession of years, and the succession of women; learned his ruthlessness, his negation of anyone and anything which interfered with his self-love and his pride.

He killed Althea. Not by neglect, not by love turned aside. By an overdose of sleeping tablets. Mike must have known that morning; even as she comforted him, she must have known she nursed a murderer at her bosom. She had known Althea. She had known Althea would not kill herself.

That she had not faced the knowledge in the days of his superb grief, was her guilt. She knew but the knowledge could not raise in her consciousness because she wanted Althea to go and him to remain. Because he was hers; for good or evil he was hers.

When she realized, it was too late. No one had suspected him, he planned too well for that. There was no one she could tell the story; she could do nothing but go on as before. She could even scoff at it as a story, an old tale dreamed by an old wife. But in the lucidity of her lone hours at night she knew. Until time faded the knowledge.

It had been years since she remembered Althea. Until yesterday with Kitten, when the name came to her lips. She sat now in her neat, compact compartment and she remembered. Remembered and was afraid.

—6—

The bride whispered to the bridegroom, "It's a beautiful world, darling."

He said, "Yes, darling, it's a beautiful world."

—7—

Mrs. Shellabarger said to her knitting and Mr. Shellabarger, "Did you see that girl who got on just ahead of us? The one with the blonde hair and mink coat? That was Kitten Agnew."

Mr. Shellabarger said to the *Readers' Digest* and Mrs. Shellabarger, "Mmph."

TWO

THE BUZZER WOKE JAMES Cobbett. He'd been sleeping with his eyes open; he'd learned how long ago. He looked up at the call box. Drawing room A. It was Vivien Spender. Too early for drinks. He rose without haste, walked the few steps to the door, tapped quietly. "Porter, sir."

"Come in." Spender didn't shout; his voice was raised just loud enough to carry. Everything in proper proportion even his voice.

Cobbett opened the door. "Yes, sir."

When he'd first gone to work on the Chief, he'd been cheerful on a call. It hadn't been for economic reasons; it was because he liked people, clean, happy people, and most persons traveling were vacation-clean and happy. He was a friendly, happy person himself. Despite the grievous weight of evidence to the contrary, he had believed that this time his happiness would be met on its own level. The Chief would be different, because it was the Chief, the best train.

It was no different. The disappointment was greater this time because he'd expected better things. The bigoted, the vulgar, the ignorant, rode the Chief as well as the lesser trains. In his first hurt, he turned sullen. That too passed because he was not dispositionally attuned to the attitude. Just as many others before and with him, he adopted the safe measure. He patronized. Unless he knew the traveler from previous runs and had accepted him as worthy of acceptance, he did not lower the bars between attendant and client. He was as aloof as an English butler.

His eye rested on Vivien Spender now without reaction. The room was unused, even the newspaper Spender had brought aboard was still neatly folded. The man himself was seated by the window. He might have been seated behind a fine desk in a pristine office; he was as emotionless as Cobbett himself.

He said, "My secretary, Miss Dana, is in the next car rear, compartment E. Would it be possible for you to send word to her that I'd like to see her?"

Cobbett said, "Yes, Mr. Spender. I'll do it." This briefly he liked Vivien Spender. It was on face valuation, he liked the smile the man gave him, a straight smile and a straight thank you. Spender hadn't come to his position through lottery. He was aware of human beings and of human values. Spender recognized his high place, Cobbett's low one in the great scheme. But he recognized a person before a position.

Cobbett closed the door. He covered the long swaying corridor, went through the vestibules into the next car. Rufus Green, attendant, was standing at the linen closet. Cobbett said, "Vivien Spender wants his secretary, Rufe. She's in E."

Rufus had a toothy grin. "That's the way the luck runs, James. You get Vivien Spender, I get the secretary."

Cobbett grinned back.

"Awright boy. I'll tell her."

Cobbett returned to his leather seat. The desert was still passing outside the windows. Be time for dinner soon. He ate at four o'clock. That way he was back in time for the cocktail bell activity.

He lifted his eyes at the opening sound of the vestibule door at the other end of the car. His glance was reflex action, nothing more. Without expression he watched the woman approach. She was a homely woman, smartly styled. Her face was gaunt, her dark hair was pulled back with severity, her lipstick matched her nails. Her suit was dark, expensive, and her green-stoned pin at her collar was handsome. Her large black handbag was handsome. She wore slant green-rimmed glasses on her eyes. Her heels were high. She gave Cobbett a casual glance.

He wasn't surprised that she knocked at Vivien Spender's door. She had the look of a secretary, a high-priced secretary. The door closed behind her. James Cobbett looked out again at the monotony of landscape.

The opening click of a door again turned his eyes. It was the other drawing room and the blonde movie actress was coming out. She hesitated a moment when she saw him sitting there. His face didn't express it but he was surprised when she knocked on the compartment next, F. That was the solitary man, the unpleasant little man. He must have called for her to enter because she opened the door and stepped in. The door didn't close at once but Cobbett didn't hear what was said. He was too far away.

A buzzer rang. Compartment D. It wasn't too unexpected. A man carrying a load such as the man who'd come back with Augustin after lunch wouldn't wait till five o'clock for another drink. Cobbett went to answer.

Within drawing room A, Mike Dana said, "You can't do it, Viv."

"I'm doing it."

She knew danger signals, the stone in his voice, the tightening of his nostrils. Openly it did not disturb her. She repeated calmly, "You can't do it. She'll break you."

"She won't break me. She'll never break me."

Mike lit a cigarette from her pocket case. She said, "Listen to me. She has you cold. And she's not bluffing. She has Seager behind her."

He swore virulently.

"All right. He's all of that. But he's the hottest lawyer in Southern California and you won't be able to beat the case."

I warned you to be careful. I've warned you over and again that someday you'd have to face judgment. You can't sin and not pay. If you sin, judgment may be delayed but not forever; the day of judgment is inevitable.

She said aloud, "Why don't you let her play Clavdia!"

He interrupted viciously, "Let that rotten little slut play Clavdia!"

"You've taught her to act. When you get down to cases, what was Clavdia but a high class slut? Kitten is boxoffice—"

He closed the subject. "She will never touch Clavdia."

And you'll never produce your masterpiece. Not even now when it's ready for production. You've waited too long. The search for the Grail was authentic at first; now it's a hunting license. You won't give up the hunt. You grow older, the Clavdias grow younger. You need their replenishment. This new one, whatever her name is, wherever you found her, will go the way of the others. She may play Cressida, she may play Corrinne Wintersmoon, but she won't play Clavdia. Someone in pigtails who has never heard of you, who is sewing doll dresses at this moment, will be the new Clavdia when this new one is old.

Mike said, "You can't take a chance on it, Viv. Not on the heels of L'Affaire Doumel."

"I'm no Doumel."

"No." He wasn't but he was. He was too close to himself to see his reflection. "The Doumel case would damn you even if she didn't have documentary evidence." Mike Dana had a calm exterior always. But she saw the frosting of his eyes and she put it away to plead, "Don't do it, Viv. Don't take a chance like that.

You have too much to live for." She realized almost with horror that she was pleading for him not to do what lay deep under the layers of his brain. Something that she had known he was considering when she saw the prescription bottle in his desk. She went on, "You'll never get to produce it if you let her get up on a witness stand."

He smiled now. "Just type the memorandum, Mike. That's all you need do. Type it and bring it to me. I'll take care of the rest."

She closed the small notebook, replaced it and her pencil in her envelope bag. "Suppose after she sees it, she still refuses your offer to buy the contract?"

He said, "If she's fool enough to turn down an amicable cool million—" He shrugged.

Mike didn't look at him. "You'll let her take it to court."

The smile was static on his lips. "She'll never play Clavdia. Never." His eyes opened wide on Mike. She backed away to the door as he ground the words, "She had the unmitigated gall to suggest I marry her."

He didn't even know when Mike opened the door, and closed it, leaving him alone, a murderer.

She stood outside a moment in the swaying corridor. There was something she ought to do. It wasn't reasonable to go away as if evil were not in that room. She should go back in, tell Viv Spender she knew what he was planning, tell him he couldn't get away with it. If he knew someone was conscious of his fearful plan he wouldn't dare do it. For he wouldn't attempt it unless he was certain he would not be detected, certain it could be foolproof. As it was the first time.

He wouldn't dare repeat the first. One could be accidental. Two would rough in the pattern, two would accuse him after fourteen years. She should go to Kitten, warn her. Mike held no brief for Kitten. The girl was a self-centered nonentity who had come to her fame and fortune through accident of a certain gamin piquancy at a moment when Viv was surfeited with cool Grecian beauty. Kitten Agnew had used her luck solely to be-diamond herself; if she'd ever had a generous impulse she'd been careful not to give way to it unless it was to her further advantage. All the stuff cooked up for her by the publicity department was accepted only because Kitten's appearance on the screen was of a warm-hearted, lovable, American girl.

Despite everything that Kitten was, she didn't deserve death. At the hands of a righteous guardian angel, perhaps yes; but not at the hands of the man who'd abetted her moral delinquency. Kitten must be given a chance to escape death.

Mike knew Kitten's space; she herself had made the arrangements. The Pullman porter wasn't in sight. There would be no one to let slip to Viv Spender that she'd visited Kitten. Viv wouldn't be prowling the corridor; not until he had his false face adjusted again. Rage had set it awry.

While Mike waited for answer to her tap, a door below her opened. She stood rigid, turned her eyes over her shoulder slowly. It wasn't Viv. It was an old man, very neat and gray, a trifle stooped. He passed her murmuring, "Excuse me."

She tapped again at drawing room B. The door was opened but it wasn't Kitten who opened it. It was a slight, dark-haired girl with star eyes in the loveliest face she'd ever looked upon. She knew who it was without knowing the name. It was the new Clavdia Chauchat.

—2—

Mike said, "May I come in?"

"Why—why certainly." The girl's voice was as beautiful as her face. It wasn't the whisky baritone affected by all the glamorous ones. It was soft and sweet and there were chimes ringing beneath it.

The girl didn't know who Mike was. He'd kept this one from every knowing person, even from Mike. But what was she doing in Kitten's drawing room? Something cold twitched Mike's fingers.

The girl stood there, quite simply, waiting for Mike to explain her reason for asking entrance. Her forefinger was tucked between the pages of the book, the little book covered in faded green. The book that Mike had given him so long ago, before he was great and strong and ruthless, when he was Viv Spender, a punk kid with dreams. So very long ago.

Mike looked around the drawing room. "Kitten isn't here? I wanted to see her. I'm Mike Dana."

The girl didn't say anything but her gray eyes with their strange purple shadows were reading Mike as if she were a small faded green book.

"Mr. Spender's secretary," Mike added. She had to say something, she felt just a little embarrassed; she, Mike Dana, embarrassed.

"I know, Miss Dana." The girl wasn't embarrassed.

Mike said suddenly, "See here, this is Kitten Agnew's drawing room, isn't it?"

"Yes, Miss Dana. She isn't here now. She went to call on a friend." She broke off, gave a small laugh. "You're wondering why I'm in here? Miss Agnew asked me to share her space to New York when Mr. Spender decided to take me along to the premiere." Her eyes were shining in anticipation.

Mike didn't laugh out loud. Kitten sharing was a dream one. The publicity department must have had an extra reefer to nightmare that one. And then she didn't want to smile. Because the publicity department wouldn't have dared; those orders came from Viv. And Viv wouldn't be escorting two Clavdias to the premiere. It was one at a time to Viv.

Mike smiled, "If you're working for Viv Spender, we ought

to know each other." Without invitation she seated herself. She looked up brightly. "I don't even know your name."

"I'm Gratia Shawn." The girl sat down opposite her.

"Not bad."

Gratia cocked her head, then understood. "It's my real name, Miss Dana."

"Make it Mike. No one calls me Miss Dana but my banker. Have you been in pictures long, Gratia?"

"I've never been in a picture." She was humble.

"Stage?"

"No." She smiled. "I was taking a library course at the university. Part of the work is assisting in the library. He came for a book. I didn't know who he was. Even when he told me his name, I didn't know. Not until one of the other librarians told me. I'm from Newfoundland."

"I've never known anyone from Newfoundland." Mike widened her eyes and her mouth. "Smoke?"

"No, thanks. I don't."

"How do you get to Hollywood from Newfoundland?" she demanded.

Gratia Shawn had lovely laughter. "A friend of mine was going. I could live with her family. So my family let me go along."

Mike asked carefully, "What does your family think of your wonderful luck?"

Gratia said quietly, "I haven't told them yet. I'm not going to tell them unless it comes to something. My friend's family agrees with me. There's no reason to set high their hopes unless I make good." She said humbly, "I don't know anything about acting on the screen. Mr. Spender says it won't be hard for me to learn. But I might not be able to learn." She laid the book across her dark dress. "If I'm not successful, I don't want them to know."

Mike eyed the book. "Like it?"

"It's wonderful. I'd always meant to read it but somehow I never got around to it before." She lifted her eyes. "Mr. Spender asked me to read it on the trip."

"Yes," Mike sighed. But Gratia didn't recognize the sigh. It was too well sublimated to the important action of putting out the cigarette. She said dryly, "I won't keep you from your reading." She went to the door. "Tell Kitten," she put her hand on the knob, "there's some stuff from the publicity department I want her to see when she has time."

She went out closing the door silently. She stood there a moment. After this share-the-space movement, the publicity department angle ought to fetch Kitten running. As well as be excuse in case Gratia mentioned the visit to Viv. He must be mad. Gratia Shawn wasn't someone he could use and discard; she was a normal, healthy person from a decent family. She was well-born. It was in every word, every slight movement.

For the moment reason faltered. It could be that Viv actually had found his Clavdia. The girl was certain to be a sensation. Yes, she would be a sensation. But she wouldn't play Clavdia Chauchat. Wearily the routine unreeled in Mike's mind. You must have some experience first, you can learn on this production. A second picture: this is a perfect gem for you, we'll postpone the other for a while. And so.

Again Mike wanted to return to Viv, to face him with reason, to force him to sanity. But she remembered the fury of his voice and face. She would speak to Kitten first. As she started towards her own car, she heard an opening door, a flurry of laughter, the laughter of men and the laughter of Kitten. Mike walked straight ahead. She didn't know why she was stewing over Kitten. Kitten wasn't worried. She was having her usual merry-making; she wouldn't appreciate having a pall hung over it. She'd be the first to say she could take care of herself.

—3—

Kitten had stepped inside the compartment too quickly. The man on the seat wasn't Les Augustin. It was a man with sleazy rayon socks slithering down to his ankles. Below the ankles were long, thin shoes, two-toned tan leather, spotted with perforations. She didn't know why anyone would have bought those shoes. But out of the past, so far away it was almost beyond memory, she did know. He had bought them because they were cheap.

He was cheap. He was dumpy and sallow, his receding hair was black furze on his pale head. No matter how much sun he took, he would never glow with tan. A tenement-soiled pallor was inlaid in his skin. His tan suit was cheap stuff, crinkled where he had rested against it. Cheap as his shoes and socks. He blinked up at her, tears of oozy self-pity, in his eyes. She blinked down at him, wondering what he was doing in a compartment on the Chief, wondering what had led her into his compartment.

And then, because she was Kitten Agnew and because he might possibly be an exhibitor from Cowpatch, Arkansas, she gave him the Kitten Agnew smile of gaiety. "I'm sorry. I picked the wrong race."

He said, "It's all right." He smiled at her. It wasn't much of a smile, it was too sad for that. "For a moment I thought maybe you'd come in here on purpose."

He couldn't be trying a verbal pass; he had a mirror, he'd know he wasn't the type. Though men never knew. Whatever he meant, she was curious. "Why did you think that?"

He debased himself. "Because you're Vivien Spender's—"

She interrupted harshly. "Go on, say it." But she didn't say it. It was an ugly word. She said, "Girl friend."

"I was going to say his number one actress."

"Like hell you were." If she was out at New Essany, she didn't have to keep up the girl-graduate act. "Who are you?"

"I'm Sidney Pringle." He waited for applause. She supposed she should give it, but she didn't have any idea what for. Broken-down actor, she labeled him.

"Won't you sit down, Miss Agnew?" Only then did he remember to rise.

"Just for a moment." She didn't know why she sat down, accepted a cigarette. He was a revolting little man. Yet the words came from her mouth, telling her why. "So you're another Spender fugitive."

He thought her words were deliberate slur. Yet he swallowed them, licked them and swallowed them, seasoning his self-pity with them. "I worked for him for some months, if that's what you mean."

"What pictures were you in?"

"I'm not an actor!" He had a shrill laugh, edgy, as if he were rusty at laughter. "I'm Sidney Pringle." He preened his fuzzy black semicircle of hair. "A writer."

"Oh." She didn't know any writers, not while they were writers alone. When they became hyphenates, when they entered the production end, she met them. "You've been writing for Viv; now he's terminated you."

"That isn't strictly true." He was obsequious. "He didn't even know I was there actually. I was hired through departments."

"And fired."

"Yes, I was fired." Resentment quivered the bulbous tip of his nose. "I didn't suit New Essany. I wasn't good enough for them. I was a worker. I didn't have a Cadillac car and a private secretary and—"

She was getting out of this. He might start throttling her with those twitching fingers because she was New Essany. She saw now the tears of pity were functional, to water his bitter anger. She stood up. "I'd like to help you but—" She might as well say it, it wouldn't be a secret much longer. "Viv Spender and I haven't been speaking for months. One word from me and he'd blackball you at all the lots." She was at the door and something about the man made her gentle. His very physical offensiveness was pathetic. "If we were speaking, I might tell him that I was delighted he'd kicked you out. That might do some good. If I get a chance I'll do it, Mister."

He was hugging despondency again. "It wouldn't do any good. He doesn't know I exist."

She made a quick exit. No more of that! She swayed alone with the corridor for a moment trying to recall which was Les Augustin's compartment. He'd mentioned it last night at the Players—it wasn't F. It came back to her. D. Compartment D. F was the compartment in Wahakatchee which that radio director had. She'd mixed them up. Both had invited her to drop in for a drink. She passed E, rapped at D.

"Come on in." That bellow couldn't be Les. But she was certain of compartment D. "Come in."

She remained on the threshold after opening the door. No more sessions with broken-down scribblers. She had enough problems of her own; she didn't need those of other persons. What she needed was escape from problems. That was her purpose in seeking Les, he was always good for diversion.

When she saw his blonde laziness on the Pullman seat she stepped in. She caroled, "Hello, duck. I came." Her eyes slanted at the man by the window, the one who was pinning her with his eyes. He was the longest, gangliest man; he had a lean, ugly face, rumpled brown hair, glazed eyes, but he was definitely aware.

Les said with his customary boredom, "Kitten, pet. I was just wondering how long."

The man at the window growled, "Don't you believe a word of it. He hasn't given you a thought."

"Shut up, Hank." Leslie didn't disturb the evenness of his

well-modulated voice. "Kitten, beloved. This is Hank Cavanaugh. He's drunk."

"Kitten is a gruesome name," Les said to Hank. "Viv Spender gave it to her."

Kitten smiled, "You're always so wonderful, Les."

She swayed from the hips as she came over to the men. She pushed in beside Les, where she could face the other. Maybe the trouble was she had been too faithful to Viv. In Cynarian fashion. If she were in love, she wouldn't have the bad dreams she had been having. Hank Cavanaugh offered something tonic.

Hank said, "If Les is in your way, he'll move. Though he'll point out selfishly that this is his compartment." He lidded his eyes at Les. "Who's the pretty thing?"

Les patted her thigh. "This is Kitten Agnew, Hank, and I've no intention of moving. Where's Viv? Skulking in his tent?"

She trickled laughter. "You're divine. He probably is." But she didn't like the switch. Skulking was a word with shadows.

"What are you afraid of?" Hank demanded.

"Nothing." She lashed her eyes at him.

"Listen kid. I've covered enough trouble to know."

Les moved in gently. "Now that you're about to play the charming consumptive, you have first-night jitters."

She edged her eyes to Les. "It looks like I'm keeping my health."

It was no surprise to him. He'd heard rumors; he wanted it first hand. He rolled it around his brain. "You have a contract."

She smiled. "I have a contract. Good till hell freezes over."

Hank said, "You're afraid of a cold snap in hell."

"I told you. I'm not afraid." She flung it at him. She wouldn't be intimidated again.

"I'm getting sober," Hank complained. "Why don't we have a straight one, Les? The dame wants one."

Les said, "What's your rush? Cobbett will have the mixings in a minute."

"Who is Cobbett, darling?"

Hank said, "Cobbett is the gentleman who attends this car. Probably the only gentleman in the car. God knows, Les isn't one."

She smiled. "Doubtless you're right. Viv Spender isn't one." She looked up at Les. "Speaking of gentlemen, I invaded the wrong compartment. I went in F." She shuddered delicately.

"Interesting."

"Hardly. The most revolting little oaf tried to weep on my shoulder. He's just been fired from New Essany. An author— Sidney Priggle or Pringle."

Hank said, "Sidney Pringle wrote a pretty good book."

She opened her eyes in simulated admiration of Hank's knowledge. "Actually? He did? I mean he really did?" But she was wary of him now.

Hank said, "Yeah." He closed his eyes again as if she didn't exist. His mouth was drawn in grim lines, too many late nights or too much trouble. He didn't belong here in Les's compartment; he was a hardbitten man, not a lazy posturer as was the great Augustin. Les was a house pet, a sleek, lazy cat; this man was lean and hungry, something out of deep woods, something cruel and lost. That was pretty good. Viv had taught her to think in pictures that way. Viv had taught her plenty of lessons; she was going to teach him one now.

She let Les play with her finger while she watched the closed eyes of Hank Cavanaugh. She asked, "Are you both going through to New York?"

"Positively," Les smiled. "No more geraniums for another year, thank God."

Hank said in a monotone, "I'm going to New York. I'm going to write a book. It'll be a whale of a book. It'll sell a million copies and I'll eat guinea hen three times a day while the people I write about go on starving. But I won't care. I won't have to watch them starve. After a while I'll have so much money I'll be able to forget them. I'll slap down a dollar when the plate is passed for relief and tell what a great humanitarian I am."

"Shut up," Les said wearily.

"Is he always like this?" she asked.

Hank answered, "Always except when he's drunk. Why don't you ask Les for a drink? He might give you one and you could slip it to me."

Les said, "It's a matter of principle, Hank. We must wait for Cobbett."

"It would be easier on the nerves if you'd pass the bottle."

She'd known Les Augustin for three years, ever since he became a name in music. She knew all the topnotchers. She gave merry, expensive parties; the successful liked parties just as much as the stragglers. Even more. She didn't like unsuccessful people. If Cavanaugh were one she must find out now. It wasn't that she was a snob about labels; it was merely that the unsuccessful, those climbing up and those falling down, were unsure, pathetic. They frightened her.

She had been safe with Les from the beginning. He was too selfish ever to fail. All the colony liked him. He was wickedly amusing on parties and he was restful. Just being with him was relaxing. How such a limp person could make the most frenetic music of the present day was always good for space in the columns. Les admitted that he hoarded his energy for performance. His other hours were spent reclining.

She couldn't understand where Hank Cavanaugh fitted with Les. She couldn't place Hank Cavanaugh in any familiar pattern. Cavanaugh didn't look like a success story; his suit was as rumpled as that of the man in compartment F, the difference was that he didn't care. He had no outward aspects of success but no inner properties of failure. He didn't seem to care about anything.

Les might have adopted him in the club car, an Augustinian gesture. Out of monkey curiosity. But there was more than casual relationship here. These men were not strangers; they had known each other a long time. She realized then that in the printed publicity of Augustin there were wide gaps. The boy genius, the Juilliard scholar, the Augustin Stomp—Hank Cavanaugh belonged in one of the gaps.

She was ready to question but there was a tap on the door.

Hank blinked open his eyes. "There's the St. Bernard." He bellowed, "Come in. Come on in."

Charles, the club-car waiter, young, handsome, grave-faced, entered. Everyone who traveled the Chief, and who was anyone, knew Charles.

Kitten smiled her smile. "Hello, Charles."

Charles said, "Hello, Miss Agnew. Mr. Augustin."

Les lifted his hand. "Hello there. Put them on the table, will you, Charles?"

"I'm Hank Cavanaugh," Hank said. "And you're a life-saver." He was holding out a bill.

Les said, "I'm host."

"The set-ups are on me," Hank growled. "I'll drink your royal booze while I'm here but I won't take your filthy lucre."

Charles set up a tray table, deposited the set-ups, the bottles of soda. "I only brought two glasses, Mr. Augustin. James said two."

"They didn't expect me," Kitten admitted. She smiled her smile again. "Though I was invited."

"I'll bring another."

Hank said, "Don't bother. I prefer the bottle."

"There's a tumbler in my room. We'll get it, Charles."

He took the bill from Hank.

Les said, "Next time you've another order this way, bring us a few more. Thanks, Charles."

The boy closed himself out.

Hank said, "If you two will kindly move your assorted legs, I'll pour. Get out your bottle, Les."

Les stirred his legs. Kitten moved hers slowly, delightfully. Les looked at Kitten. "Go get Kitten's tumbler, Hank, while I open the quart." His slim hand closed on hers. "Hank needs the exercise, pet. And I need you." She was watching Hank, but she knew the look in Les's eyes didn't match his voice.

Hank rose grumpily. "Where the hell do I go? Compartment F?"

"No," she warned. "That's Pringle or Priggle. I'm drawing room B." She pointed. "That way. The tumbler's in the bath cabinet."

Hank growled, "I warn you I shall return." He banged the door.

Les opened a valise.

She leaned back, lazily. "Why did you deliberately give him the wrong impression?"

He lifted out the pinch bottle. "What's up, Kitten? What are you afraid of?" He spoke as she opened her mouth. "What's up with you and Viv?"

It couldn't be that it was so obvious. He was fishing, with Hank Cavanaugh's shot in the dark for bait.

She shrugged. "I'm not afraid."

"You're an E string turned too tight."

"Don't be poetic." She moved over to the window. "I've been working too hard. I need a vacation."

"A long one?" He measured Scotch into the glass.

She said, "Viv and I are through. But I don't have to worry. I have contracts, and a lawyer. He can't throw me out. Either I play Clavdia, or he doesn't produce his masterpiece."

Les tossed his head and laughed. "You mean there's a new one."

She held out her fingers for the drink. "I mean there won't be a new one." She smiled.

Her smile covered her inward tremors. Viv had never been thwarted since he came to power. He wouldn't be thwarted. But he couldn't stop her. Only by death.

She wasn't coming back from New York. Her ticket was marked one way. Gratia Shawn had a round-trip ticket. The conductors hadn't thought it strange when they checked the tickets. Gratia hadn't noticed.

She took a drink. "Did you ever hear about Viv's wife?" It wasn't what she wanted to talk about; she'd come here to forget. But Les collected odd scandals; in his ragbag brain there might be a scrap of information.

"You mean Viv's married?"

"He was once. Years ago."

"I never knew he'd been married. What about her?"

She said, "I don't know about her. I never heard about her until this week. She's dead." She sipped. He couldn't know it was tasteless. "He's never mentioned her."

Les said, "Maybe he still grieves." He knew it was absurd. "Who told you? Mike?"

"Yes," she admitted reluctantly. He'd go to Mike. She shouldn't have spoken. But it didn't matter really; he'd be off-hand, casual. Les was clever and careful. His ferreting might bring to light more information. She switched the subject. "Who is Hank Cavanaugh?"

"Newspaperman."

"You've known him a long time." She made it statement.

"Yes. I knew him in New York when he was just another reporter."

She was curious. "What is he now?"

"He's a big shot. He's won a lot of medals on his stuff."

She slanted her eyes.

"He was a war correspondent. Was in Singapore before Pearl Harbor. He's just back from China." Leslie was strangely thoughtful. "He must have cracked up over something. The drinking—"

She said, "Is he broke?"

"No. He can't afford you but he isn't broke."

"He looks it."

Leslie smiled. "He always looks that way." He settled himself. "Tell me your troubles, darling. That's what you came for, isn't it?"

"Definitely not. I came to be amused. To forget. Tell me a story. About you and Hank Cavanaugh."

His eyes slitted. "You're not serious."

"What do you mean?"

"About Hank." He tittered. "Oh no, Kitten!"

"Why not?" She rounded her mouth thoughtfully. "Three days and nothing to do. Anything can happen in that time."

"Anything can," he agreed pleasantly. "Except making hay with Hank Cavanaugh."

"A Krister or—"

"Neither." He frowned quickly. "Something's happened to him. All he wants is to stay drunk."

"Perhaps I could help him forget." She was amused. But that was only for Les. Hank was all right. Hank could keep her from thinking. And he could keep her from being alone; if she weren't alone, Viv couldn't get at her. The starry-eyed bookworm wasn't any protection; Viv could use a machine gun and Gratia Shawn would think it was in the contract.

Les coaxed. "I wish you'd tell me about it. Maybe I could help out."

It wasn't to lend a helping hand that he wanted to know. It

was his greedy curiosity, the desire to be first on all scandals. If she told him, the story would be hawked in the Cub room Saturday night, whispered at the Wedgwood room, shouted at Copa. She'd be a laughing stock, the girl who thought Viv Spender was a gunsel. That might be a way to tie his hands. A small quaver warned her against belief. It would only make Viv more careful in his plannings. The point was not to be alone with him.

She said, "There's nothing to tell, Les. Truly. He's going to try to give me the brush-off but he's going to find he can't do it." Her mouth set hard. "For once he's going to have to fulfill a promise. I don't look forward to the battle but I can't lose." Only by death. She lashed her eyes that Les couldn't see the fear again. "I wonder what's happened to your friend Cavanaugh."

Les laughed lazily. "We probably won't see him again until we reach Chicago. You'd better put up with me, darling."

—4—

He was too sober. He stood in the corridor and the corridor swayed but he was steady. He didn't have to go to the blonde's compartment and pick up her damn tumbler; he could walk straight along into the next car. Keep walking until he reached the club car. He knew what to do when he reached it. He could stop his mind from functioning; he'd learned how.

Les didn't want him to return. Les wanted to be alone with the blonde hussy. Hank didn't give a damn about her; let Les pick her brains, find out what made her afraid. He didn't care. The days when he'd tried to beat Les to the details of a yarn were long past, thank God.

If he weren't too sober he wouldn't have seen the fear Kitten was trying to keep covered. Even if he'd seen it, he wouldn't have cared. It wouldn't be nagging at him now when he should be moving one foot after another towards the bar.

What had a girl like Kitten to fear? She wasn't smart enough to be aware of the big things, the mad chaos of the spheres. She wasn't facing want, one look at her dispelled that fantasy. She wasn't old enough to fear the creeping debility of oncoming age. Fear of losing love? He scoffed the idea; there was nothing dewy-eyed about Kitten.

It wasn't any small fear eating her; it was something basic, something terrorizing. One look and he'd recognized it. Because he hadn't seen anything much but fear in these last years. He shook his head. He mustn't remember; he must not remember. He must stay drunk. But he didn't walk forward in the train. He flung open the door of drawing room B. Flung it open, despising himself for his curiosity about a tinsel doll, for expecting blood when there could be nothing but sawdust.

The train lurched and he fell into the room muttering about damn trains and damn curves and damn tumblers and God-damn blondes. He didn't see the girl until he'd closed the door. She wasn't a blonde. She wasn't tinsel.

She was seated by the window, her finger marking a place in her book. Her eyes were lifted to him, not so much in curiosity as in wonderment. He brushed the hair out of his eyes, the first time in years. And he damned himself silently after his hand fell. Did he think she'd see the Hank Cavanaugh who once was, simply because his hair was in place? He knew what she'd see: a gaunt scarecrow, his face riddled with fatigue and anger, not trivial emotions of the moment, but of long standing. Did he care what she'd see? Not a tinker's dam.

He demanded rudely, "Who're you?"

She answered simply, "I'm Gratia Shawn."

He stood there blank and silent. What did he expect her to say? *Lie here and rest. Try to forget.* Because there was serenity in her face, because he could find peace in her, didn't mean she had been put down here for that purpose. He must be drunker than he thought. Yet he had never felt more sober. It was a long time since he had felt as secure.

He said, "You're beautiful, Gratia Shawn."

"Am I?" She might never have heard the words before. But there was a flush of embarrassment touching her cheeks. She didn't realize he was saying nothing personal; it was as if he were looking at a painting.

"Yes. You're beautiful." He walked over to her until he stood above her and she was frightened. He didn't blame her for being frightened. He wanted to tell her not to be but it didn't seem important. He said, "You're so beautiful, it hurts. Here." He put his hand on his vest. He wasn't as sober as he'd thought. He wavered down beside her. "Who is Gratia Shawn?"

"I am." She was humoring him. Usually it angered him, but with her he didn't care. "Who are you?" she asked.

"What's the difference?"

She said, "I want to know. I told you my name. You tell me yours."

"I'm Hank Cavanaugh."

"The newspaper Cavanaugh—" Her face lighted with recognition.

His eyebrows raged. "I'm Cavanaugh, the bum. What are you doing in Kitten Agnew's room?"

"I'm going to New York."

"What for?"

"For the premiere of Kitten's new picture."

There was lovely excitement in her voice. He didn't like it. "Are you a friend of Kitten's?" he demanded.

"Oh no. I never met her until this morning." She explained, "The studio couldn't get space for me and she offered to share hers."

"You in the moving pictures?" He didn't want her to be.

She said, "N-no." Not yet.

"You want to be," he accused.

"If I can be good, yes." There was a dream in her eyes.

He said harshly, "You can't be good. They'll destroy you. They'll take away your beauty. They'll turn you into a painted hussy. Like Kitten." He broke off, "What's Kitten afraid of?"

"Afraid?" She didn't understand.

"Is she afraid of you?" He shook his head.

"Of course not." Her laugh was puzzled. "That's absurd. I'm nobody."

"It isn't that," he decided for himself. "She may be. Maybe she's smart enough for that. Probably not. But it isn't that." He said, "She's afraid. She won't admit it." He flared at her. "I know fear when I see it. I've seen it. Fear of hunger. Fear of pain. Fear of losing the ones you love. Fear of death." His eyes were suddenly clear. "She's afraid of death." He took the book from her. "Come on."

She shook her head, "No." She held out her hand for the book. "I don't want to go anywhere."

He said, "We've got to find out about Kitten."

"You go."

He pulled her to her feet. "I want you with me."

"Why?" She wasn't protesting enough. She'd go with him. If she refused, he wouldn't go. He wouldn't lose her.

"I want to look at you," he said. "Where's her Goddam tumbler?"

"That's silly." Her cheeks had warmed again.

"It isn't silly. I'm a newspaperman. I used to be anyway. I can't let a story like this pass me up. Suppose something had happened to Mary Pickford when—you're too young to understand. Suppose Shirley Temple had—" He banged open the door of the bath, came out with a red plastic glass. "If I have you to look at, maybe I won't get too drunk to keep my eye on the story. Besides I'd like to see you two together. Maybe she'll let something slip—"

He had her hand and the door open while he talked. She didn't protest again. She went with him out into the corridor, swaying the few doors to D. He opened it without knocking, pushed her in ahead of him. "Look what I found," he announced.

The fair young man and Kitten turned their heads and looked. Kitten didn't like Gratia being here, there was a quick glint in her eyes. She masked it at once, extending a friendly hand. "I'm glad you came along, Gratia." Then her eyes opened wide on Hank. "You're positively powerful. How did you ever pry her away from that book?"

"I threatened her with an ax." He was brusque with Kitten. If it weren't for Kitten, he could go away with Gratia and rest.

Les had turned languidly but when he saw Gratia his eyes became fixed. She was more embarrassed than she had been under Hank's earlier scrutiny. Hank knew why. He'd seen it happen to others. She hadn't the slightest idea what Augustin was thinking behind his silent face.

"So this is Gratia Shawn." Les's voice was gentle and amused. "I'm Leslie Augustin."

She said, "Leslie Augustin," as if she didn't quite believe it.

Les's face lighted with the candle of a smile.

Hank groaned, "Oh God."

"What's the matter now?" Les asked.

"We're still shy a glass." Hank held out the red tumbler.

Gratia sat down on the couch. "I don't care about drinking. You take it."

"You mean you don't drink?" Kitten's small laugh clawed. Gratia might have been relic of an old attic.

Gratia didn't want any trouble with Kitten. She didn't offer any resentment. She answered peaceably. "I just don't care about it."

Hank sprawled down beside Gratia. "We're sharing. I drink half." He drank half. He put the tumbler in her hand. "When you drink your half, we'll have another. Not until."

Les Augustin grimaced. "If you can hold Hank to that, you'll have to give up your screen career, Gratia. You'll have your future cut out as his guardian angel."

Kitten didn't like that either. She didn't like Hank sitting beside Gratia. She wasn't getting the attention and she demanded it. Gratia turned it quickly back to her. "Mike Dana came in to see you."

Kitten was suddenly naked. Hank looked quickly, angrily at Gratia. Her face quieted the anger. She hadn't said this with purpose to frighten Kitten. Her own eyes were wide and puzzled.

"Who's Mike Dana?" Hank demanded. But his voice was quiet.

"Mike Dana," Les smiled slantly, "is the very private secretary of our friend, Vivien Spender."

"What did she want?" Kitten might not have heard their interlude. Her eyes were great and shadowed. On Gratia.

Gratia tried to speak as if she hadn't noticed. "She wanted to see you. Something about the publicity department."

"The publicity department." Assurance was returning to Kitten. She was forcing its return. She moved her head in irritation. "Always the publicity department." She tilted her drink. "They can jolly well wait."

"That's the spirit," Les murmured. He returned his narrow eyes to Gratia. "I've never seen you before," he stated. "I'd remember you if I had. You have a face to remember."

"She's beautiful," Hank told him.

Gratia was uneasy, glancing under her eyes at Kitten. This time Kitten didn't seem to notice. She was looking out the window, looking into space because there was nothing but scrub and space outside.

"What pictures have I missed?"

Les was speaking directly to Gratia, but she didn't understand.

"In what pictures have you appeared?"

"Oh, I haven't been in any pictures," she said quickly.

"She's an unknown," Kitten said. There was meaning behind the words but Gratia couldn't read it. She didn't know enough. Kitten drained her glass. "Maybe I'd better go see Mike."

"Now?" Les protested.

"It might be important." She didn't want to go. She sat there, reluctance on her shoulders.

Hank said, "You're too slow." He took the tumbler from Gratia's fingers, drained it. "I'll go with you," he told Kitten. He didn't want to go. He didn't want to pity her, to be forced to protect her. But he was powerless. She wasn't an expensive blonde tramp; she was all the helpless, terrified women he'd been unable to protect; her eyes were their agonized pleading eyes.

Color came again into her face as he spoke. "You will?" She rose then. "Move your long legs, Les."

"You're so energetic," Les protested. He swung them aside for her to pass. "Don't be long, pet. We'll wait dinner."

"It won't take me five minutes to tell Mike what I think of the publicity department."

"And five minutes more for me to tell Mike what I think of all publicity departments," Hank grimaced. He touched Gratia's hand. She wouldn't understand what he was trying to tell her, that he didn't want to leave her and do battle; he wanted only her quiet peace. She didn't understand. She was watching Kitten. His eyes too, turned to Kitten.

At some point crossing that small room, she had changed again. He knew undeniably then that he had sensed truth; Kitten was afraid. It was fear that had stripped her of her poise at mention of Mike Dana's visit. It was fear that made her move more slowly now. He rose up from the couch to meet her. She was trying to make her smile natural when she lifted it to Hank. But her speech was nervous. "You'd better not come along after all." She curved about his arm her small hand with the long scarlet almond nails. "It's strictly business. I can finish it quicker alone." Her smile became provocation. "Be sure to wait dinner."

"You're certain you want to go alone?"

"Absolutely certain," she smiled.

He opened the door for her, watched her out of sight. When he closed the door, he questioned Les Augustin. "What's Mike Dana got on her? Why is she afraid of Mike Dana?"

Les's smile was patronizing. "She's not afraid of Mike Dana." He added fondly, "Stupid."

—5—

He had it planned. Now that it was consummated in his mind, it seemed as if he'd been planning it for a long time. As if knowledge had been there from the source that the beginning could only lead to this ultimate end. That he had known in first meeting with Kitten that she must be destroyed.

She hadn't been like any of the others. He didn't know now what it was of her that had caught his attention. There must have been something; he didn't choose without a reason. The reason was gone, lost in the penance of years in which he'd been forced to wear Kitten, a haircloth beneath his position and his pride.

He should have realized before how simple it would be to rid himself of her. He needn't have endured the nettle of her this long if he'd faced the problem before. It had taken her final blatant insult to make him face it. He was a busy man, that was the trouble; he hadn't had the time for clear thought. Not until she flung her insolent demand and he was momentarily dropped like a stone into a void of blackness. He had pushed up to the surface with the knowledge of what must be. The million-dollar gesture was only that; he knew Kitten would not settle for less than the role of Clavdia—or of Mrs. Vivien Spender. She would get neither. Kitten must die.

With the decision had come a calm he hadn't known in years, in the years of Kitten. A calm that came with lightness. It had been simple to chart the plans. It would be as simple to effect them. The only difficulty was to make certain that Gratia Shawn was out of the way. He must invent some business for Mike to take up with her during the hour.

It wouldn't hurt to have Gratia present as a witness. In case there was questioning afterwards, her innocence would favor him. But Gratia mustn't be touched even faintly with anything sordid. Better to have no witness to the deed. Not even one to testify to his honor.

It would have been wiser not to have included Gratia on the journey. He had known that when he planned it. Yet he did not regret overriding his sober judgment. It had been long since his pulses quickened, since warmth crept through his veins at mere mention of a name, the name. He couldn't resist the irresistible; he did not want to leave her behind nor did he leave her behind. She was here with him. Separated only by a few doors, and by Kitten.

He regretted now the impulse which had prompted him to have her travel with Kitten. There was ironic juxtaposition to it, yes, just as he had conceived of it. It had infuriated Kitten just as he had hoped. He smiled remembering his publicity boys' report of Kitten receiving the news. The boys in Publicity were clever; better give them a raise. Before some other studio found out how clever they were and tried to snatch them. That was the trouble with other studios. No moral sense, no respect for property. Not enough talent to make their own finds; scavenging off their betters.

His mouth tightened happily. Wait until the other studios saw what he did with Gratia Shawn. They'd all be blubbering into their Scotch. They'd all be crying anew about the genius of Viv Spender, cursing his ability to discover the rare and the exquisite. He'd sit back and smile at them; smile with pity. He'd let them knew they too could have had Gratia Shawn. She was under their eyes all the time. To be sure they might not use the great library as often as he, but that was their prerogative. If they preferred Hollypark or Ciro's to Knowledge, who was he to suggest they change their spots? The library was there with its priceless treasures. One of which was Gratia Shawn.

It was entirely possible that they might have seen in Gratia Shawn only a colorless, soft-spoken librarian. Remembering the beauty of her face, he knew this was untrue. They, any of them, would have recognized beauty. They dealt in beauty. It was likewise true that, recognizing beauty, they would not always take a chance on unknown beauty. If they had noticed Gratia Shawn, it was entirely possible they might have passed her by. Because among all of them there wasn't another Viv Spender.

Now that he had found Gratia Shawn, he would watch the lesser producers writhe. She would be his greatest star. His other discoveries, each one, had in time been proved with blemish. He had tried to make goddesses of them but they refused to give up their clumsy clay feet. He wouldn't let it happen to Gratia. He would create her as an artist created his masterpiece; he would treasure her as a precious gem. She was the perfect medium, the blank page. She had not been infected by the colony; she was without desire, without ambition. Beautiful, gentle, serious.

She had photographed breath-takingly. She didn't know; he'd withheld the tests from her. She couldn't act but he'd teach her that. Her voice was exquisite. He was a great teacher, the greatest teacher in the colony. Look what he'd done for Kitten.

The scowl ravaged his face again. Kitten. He'd made mistakes but never one of the magnitude of Kitten. His hands twitched to throttle her with his bare hands; his foot knotted to step on her as on a beetle. If civilization were more decently primitive, he could end Kitten as she should be ended. He had created her; she was bad; he should be permitted to destroy her. With violence not trickery. What had she been? A cheap little tramp dancing in a third-rate bar, singing through her nose. He'd made her more than a great star, he'd made her the pattern of a lovely woman and a fine actress. He hadn't known that the cheapness had poisoned her veins, that she'd never drain it off.

She'd had her chance. She didn't deserve another but he'd give it to her. Because he was civilized. Because he was fair. A million dollars in exchange for those papers her shyster was holding, and her signature that she wouldn't work for another studio for five years. The latter stipulation was business. He was a business man. You didn't perfect something and give it away to your competitors. He smiled coldly. In five years she would be forgotten. Those whose career depended on being before the public couldn't exist after a five-year oblivion.

If she refused his terms . . . His eyes met the eyes of the man in the mirror. She would refuse, and his plans were made. He had even prepared his speech for the reporters. "The show must go on. It is the way Kitten would have wanted it. The premiere will proceed as planned, a tribute to her courage and her art."

The man in the mirror was tall and well built. His head was leonine, his face strong and intelligent. He smiled, his smile was honest. He didn't appear to be nearing fifty. There was no touch of gray in his hair, no pouches under his clear gray eyes. He was a man who could make decisions and carry them through to firm success. He was a man who commanded the attention of men and women. A man who could make of Gratia Shawn the most glorious creature who had yet appeared on the screen. He could now produce his book; he had found Clavdia Chauchat. First she must learn of course, but it would not take her long.

He had not intended seeing Gratia while on board the Chief. He had been carefully secret of her thus far. He intended to take no chances where she was concerned. Time enough to learn her in the great crowded anonymity of New York. But the urge to look upon her face was strong. To hear her voice, to watch her move. There was no reason why he shouldn't see her; he intended to announce his find as soon as he reached New York. She couldn't be stolen now; she had signed his contract. He rang for the porter, as he rang recalling the name he'd noted when entering the car. Cobbett.

He sat there, his hands quiet, watching the handsome man in the mirror. When the knock came at the door he raised his voice correctly and watched the door open. He liked Cobbett; the man wasn't obsequious as were most attendants to the great Spender; he had dignity. Cobbett was decently interested but no more than that. The porter liked him. That was not unusual; where Viv gave liking, it was seldom not returned.

He said, "Cobbett, would you mind asking Miss Shawn, drawing room B, if she'd step in to see me?"

"Yes, sir."

The door closed. He'd like a man such as Cobbett for his secretary. Mike had always been too personal, recently she'd intensified it. True, she'd warned him of Kitten's changeless nature. But she ought not to refer to it now. It wasn't her place to remind the boss of his mistakes.

Why had he kept Mike so many years? Laziness, he told

himself sharply. No other reason. To avoid breaking in someone new. If he had someone like Cobbett he'd have the perfect secretary. Cobbett would never interfere; he would retain his aloofness. Vivien Spender amused himself with the idea while he was waiting. Cobbett was probably a college graduate; ridiculous that he should be forced to earn his living as a porter. Obviously he was qualified for a more intellectual position. If he took Cobbett for secretary, that would give the colony something to buzz about.

He couldn't kick Mike out, not after twenty-odd years. He could pension her but she wouldn't gracefully be turned out to graze. He could elevate her; everyone wanted to get into production. His hands moved slightly. There were so many fascinating things he could do. Once he was rid of Kitten.

He turned on his smile quickly at the knock on the door. "Come in." His voice was warm; perhaps a shade too loud. His veins ran warm. But it was Cobbett who again stood there.

"She isn't in her room, Mr. Spender."

"Where is she?" His frown was slight and he erased it at once. Although he had a right to annoyance. She should have been there. Gratia Shawn knew no one on the Chief.

"I don't know, Mr. Spender. There was no one there."

He smiled mechanically. "Thank you, Cobbett."

Kitten had taken Gratia on her club car maraudings. He couldn't send for Gratia now, advertise his interest to the Chief gossips. He was not a man to be thwarted. He intended to see Gratia. He would go along to the club car, join the girls casually. Invite them to dine with him. It was a good move after all; everything friendly on the surface. The great man taking Kitten and her protégée to dinner.

The train was slowing. He looked out into the twilight, then glanced down at his watch. Needles already, six forty-five. He widened his smile. This was better. He'd get off and walk, board the train again at the club car. The meeting would be accidental, no seeking out. Fate, as was her custom, played his hand.

Even Fate would not thwart Vivien Spender.

—6—

Kitten said, "What does the publicity department want now that I should do? Ride in the baggage section?"

The train was stopping at Needles. The Chief was hermetically sealed in its own air-conditioned void. No desert heat could penetrate. The sluggish men and women on the station platform stood in the heavy, unmoving air outside and gazed curiously in at the sterile faces behind the train windows.

Mike said, "Not yet." She laughed after she said it, but the laugh was too sharp; it was almost a cry. "You're a riot, Kitten. No, it's just some releases for New York I wanted you to okay."

Kitten took the typewritten pages disinterestedly. "That's the trouble with these cross-countries. No agent to do the dirty work." She looked at papers with disdain. "Do I have to read all this stuff?"

"I've read it; you don't have to," Mike said. "Just pencil on your initials."

Kitten took the pencil Mike offered. "Viv and his bureaucracy. The other studios don't go in for this red tape."

"It's for your own protection," Mike said mechanically.

She had to bring up the subject of the wife. She had to delay long enough to get Mike to talk about it. She nibbled the pencil and looked over the first page. "Maybe I'd better read them," she said. "Maybe he is trying to slip a fast one over me. Like putting that girl in my drawing room."

"How are you getting along with her?" Mike spoke absently, without interest. She was gazing out the window.

Kitten followed her gaze. She drew back. He was striding

down the platform. Viv Spender, the king. She didn't want him to see her. She didn't want a scene with him now. She wanted to get back to Hank; it wasn't safe leaving a man with Gratia Shawn.

Mike, too, had drawn back as Viv passed. Kitten's eyes were shrewd. "He's trying to put something over. What is it?"

Mike eyed her for a long moment out of her green-rimmed glasses. Her hand moved to a typewritten sheet on another sheaf of papers. She held it put silently.

Kitten took the sheet but she didn't look at it. She looked at Mike. Mike's eyes were as expressionless as the glass panes covering them. The paper was undated. Kitten read: Vivien Spender (his name must be first always) announced today that Gratia Shawn . . . Kitten crumpled the paper from her. It fell to the carpet, lay there, a white blotch.

"He isn't putting anything over on you. He told you."

Kitten asked, "When is he releasing that?" Her throat was dusty.

"When we get to New York."

"He's already signed her?"

"He says so. I haven't seen the contract."

Kitten said harshly, "He can't do it."

"I wouldn't try to stop him." Behind the slant green glasses Mike's eyes appealed to her. "He's in an ugly mood."

"So am I."

Mike cried out now, "Why not settle your contract, Kitten?" It wasn't like Mike, the unemotional, to be emotional.

It brought the fear again to Kitten's spine but she arched her anger against it. "He can't do it to me. I've got him where I want him."

Mike's voice was ragged. "Don't fight him, Kitten." It broke. "For God's sake, why would you want to marry him? He'd be a rotten husband."

He'd told Mike. And Mike had brought up the subject. Kitten said, "I wanted to be the first Mrs. Spender." Now that the opening was made, Kitten was almost afraid to move towards it. She was forced to; she must know. But she was awkward, the shadow of death lay there. "I didn't know there'd been one."

Mike didn't help; she sat motionless as the desert air outside.

Kitten spoke hushedly, as if he were listening. "Why does he never talk about it? Why does no one ever talk about her?"

Mike said heavily, "She's dead."

"You told me that. But why is it she's—" She finished slowly, "It's as if she never existed."

"He doesn't want to be reminded of her."

Kitten stood there, trying to control curiosity that was more, and less, than curiosity. Not wanting to ask, not wanting to know, yet having to seek the answer. "How did she die?" Her whisper was terrible.

Mike said in that monotone, "An overdose of sleeping tablets."

There was no implication beyond the statement, not in Mike's face nor in her shoulders nor her quiet hands and feet. There was nothing said or unsaid to frost Kitten's fingertips. Nothing to diminish her voice to whisper. "Why? Why?"

Mike touched her tongue to her lips. The words came hard. "She wasn't happy."

Kitten took a small breath. "You knew her." She realized that now. Mike had been his secretary since he first started in pictures, while he was yet an unknown. Mike had been his secretary when there was a Mrs. Spender. "What was she like?"

Before Mike answered the room was so quiet you could hear the beat of your heart.

Mike said, "She was just an ordinary woman. She liked

her home and meeting friends for lunch and going shopping, having her hair done and driving out in the Valley on Sunday afternoons. She wasn't ambitious, she just wished to be happy. She wanted children. She was very much in love with her husband."

He killed her. Kitten hadn't spoken aloud but it screamed from her throat. He killed her! She knew it now. Knew it in the way Mike had shrunk, diminished to a green pinpoint before her eyes, it was what Mike had tried to tell her yesterday. Tried but failed, because the words wouldn't come out of her mouth. The horror was like a fog before Kitten's face. She repeated, "Why, why?"

The Chief stirred. It crept away from the station so quietly it might not be moving, only giving the illusion of moving. But the faces were going away.

"It was Rosaleen." Mike didn't look at Kitten, her fingers twisted together. "He isn't like other men. He sees everything through a dream."

Kitten's voice was hard. "His dream." Bitter and hard as green fruit. "For once he's going to have to pay. Pay through the nose. He's not going to kick me out the way he did the others. Maybe you can wake him up long enough to tell him that."

She began penciling the pages rapidly.

Mike picked up the blotch from the floor, smoothed it out. She said, "I wish I could tell him."

Kitten thrust the sheaf at her. She wasn't going to think about it longer now. She knew enough to keep away from Viv Spender. There'd be no overdose of sleeping tablets for her. She rose from the seat.

"Thanks, Mike."

"Kitten—"

She turned back at the door.

Mike said only, "Be careful." It wasn't what she'd started to say.

Kitten smiled, lifted her hand in salute. But there was no smile on her face as she stood in the corridor outside the compartment. She stood a moment, then fled back to the next car as if the hooded shadow were falling over her head.

THREE

He had planned and Kitten had eluded the plan. He sat in the car tearing paper into small neat pieces. He didn't know where the paper had come from but he tore it down, across, across again until the palm of his hand was filled with the small particles.

He had watched them as they passed through the club car on their way to the diner. None of them saw him; they were too busy laughing together. In the lead Leslie Augustin and the lovely Gratia Shawn. Following the two, Kitten and a tall, seedy-looking fellow who was obviously drunk.

Gratia had no business being with Augustin. Augustin was an arrogant young whipper-snapper who played the piano or drums and who mocked at a Spender motion-picture contract. Augustin was too well known. The petty gossip spies who crawled through the train would be checking up on the girl now.

Gratia wasn't to be mentioned until she was introduced with proper fanfare by Vivien Spender. Now he'd have to go to Mike, see what she could do to silence the gossips before they could speak in print. His knuckles where white and hard. He wasn't going to have his plans for the girl upset. Not if he had to buy off every one of the scavengers of rumor.

Kitten knew he didn't want Gratia Shawn bandied around

the Chief; she must have known. It was deliberate on her part, involving the girl with the adder-tongued Augustin and an unknown drunk. Mike would have to do something about it. He hadn't suggested that Kitten keep Gratia undercover, he couldn't very well do that. But he had counted on Kitten's natural meanness. The suggestion that she look out for the girl ordinarily would have been enough to keep Gratia a nonentity for the journey.

Kitten wouldn't have been smart enough to think this up alone; Augustin must have had a hand in it. He'd warned Kitten before about Augustin's sly malice; unfortunately the band leader was fashionable and Kitten thought more of the latest fad than of good advice. Kitten evidently had told Augustin how the wind blew from Fisherman's Wharf. The papers began to trickle from Viv's hand. She wouldn't have told Augustin the whole story; she wouldn't have dared. She'd have to withhold her ammunition until the psychological moment; her crook lawyer would insists on that.

It would be Augustin who would realize that flaunting Gratia openly would twist a knife in Spender. Not that Augustin had anything against Viv Spender; only that he enjoyed experimenting with knives. He'd break Augustin yet. There'd be a way; he'd find the way. The fair-haired boy was increasingly irritating.

That much of the picture was clear. The drunk with Kitten wasn't. Kitten was usually too proud in her public appearances. Yet she'd been looking up at that fellow as if he were someone important. Where had she found him? And where had she and Gratia been for the past hours?

They'd been laughing. They'd walked by him as if he were a hardware salesman, without seeing him. He opened his hand and the confetti spilled to the carpet. He was ready to rise when he saw Mike winding through the aisle, skirting the long legs of someone on the couch by the entrance.

Mike saw Viv and she stopped in front of his chair. Her face had been sober when she appeared in the car. The brightness that came to it when she saw him wasn't natural. It was as if she'd pressed a button forcing it to light.

She asked, "Whatever brought you in here, Boss?"

He flashed a good smile. "I came down with claustrophobia. Took a walk at Needles and had to jump on. Have a drink?"

"No, thanks. I'm after food." She started away but he stopped her by rising.

"How about joining me for dinner? Now that I'm here, I might as well try the diner."

"You won't like it," she warned. "It's full of people."

"Tonight I like people. I'm observing them. Research."

They could smile at each other because they'd known each other a long time, long enough that each could respect the other's cloak of pretense. Mike wasn't easy; maybe she knew what Kitten was up to, was trying to spare him. She didn't want him to go into the diner; even now that he was urging her forward, she was hesitating.

He said, "I mustn't lose the common touch, Mike. You can't sit on Olympus and direct the American street scene."

"I thought you were planning to sit on the Schwarzhorn."

"Don't quibble."

The steward didn't know Vivien Spender. The steward was a small man, suave, impersonal. He said, "Two? This way." The table to which he led them was already occupied by a middle-aged couple, facing forward. Mike slid into the window seat, Spender sat beside her. He'd asked for the common touch; he'd accept it gracefully, dining backwards opposite the dullness of strangers.

Gratia's face was framed for him through the intervening heads. He was gratified that she didn't seem a part of her group. She smiled when their laughter rattled but she was silent otherwise, careless of Les Augustin at her side, watching Kitten and the man across the table. She didn't see Viv Spender, she wasn't looking in his direction. There was a table separating this table from that of Kitten's party.

The man across from Viv leaned forward confidentially. "That's Kitten Agnew back there," he said.

Viv nodded. "Yes, I know." He made himself look and sound interested.

The woman beside the man, the woman in the dowdy, expensive dress, smiled complacently. "She's Dad's favorite actress."

"What I like about her," the man defended, "is she's a real American girl." He went on about it in many words. The look on Viv's face was a listening one. He supplied a variety of sounds when the monologue demanded it. God, the public really believed that stuff! The publicity department had told Viv so but he'd never quite credited it. One look at Kitten and you knew her beginnings and her probable end if she lived to that end. But the public wasn't as discerning as Viv Spender.

And how would the public accept Kitten's death before the end? They wouldn't like it. How would they accept her producer going on to New York, making sure the show would go on as Kitten wanted it to go on? They'd accept it; they'd accept it because the whole sticky sweet mess would be spoon fed them by the boys in Publicity. He had no intention of missing the premiere. His fingers tightened and he said, "Yes indeed," to the man across the table.

"Did you see her in *Fancy That?*" The garrulous fellow was launched again. He was even humming tunelessly the theme song, "Fancy That." Kitten had done it well. It had been a good picture, a picture she could do. The story of a girl who wanted to be a successful singer, who almost got there, but who decided she didn't really want it after all. Who turned her back on fame and fortune when it was within her grasp. Who chose instead the boy she loved and a little rose-covered cottage. Pure hoke and the public loved it. As far from Kitten's nature as simple goodness and the public loved her.

The picture had grossed a mint. Kitten could go on doing that sort of thing until she became a character actress and keep on grossing six figures. If she only had brains enough to realize that hoke was her fortune, not want to mangle Clavdia Chauchat. He'd made a mistake thinking she was Clavdia; he admitted it, why couldn't she? He wouldn't have dropped Kitten if she'd been reasonable. He'd have kept her on; she could have remained right there at the top for years to come.

It was too late now. She'd refused reason; she'd threatened. And she'd mouthed the unforgivable insult, she'd demanded marriage.

Mike touched his arm. "What are you ordering, Viv?"

He looked at the menu, quieting the twitch of his hands. It might have been that Mike knew his mind. He smiled secretly. She couldn't this time. He hadn't told her anything. She didn't know anything about Gratia Shawn, nothing except the dictation she'd taken this afternoon, the announcement that Gratia Shawn would play the part of Clavdia Chauchat in Vivien Spender's production. Mike hadn't even seen the girl. He'd got her aboard without Mike knowing. Mike wasn't as indispensable as she thought.

She said, "I'll take the steak."

He ordered for them. The couple across left the table. It brought Gratia's face into frame. He couldn't resist. He said quietly, "That's Gratia Shawn."

"Yes, I know."

Yes, she knew. He'd just congratulated himself that she didn't know and she knew. He was pricked and he scowled at her. "How is it you know? She's never been on the lot."

"I met her this afternoon."

He was sharp. "How?"

Mike was removing a cigarette from her black handbag. Her voice was easy. "I went to ask Kitten to o.k. the publicity for New York. That girl was in the drawing room."

He wanted Mike to talk about her, to react to her, but she was silent.

He was forced to ask, "Lovely, isn't she?"

"Yes," Mike said.

He burned silently. Mike mustn't be allowed to think he had any interest in the girl save professionally. Actually he hadn't. He'd treated her like a daughter. If within him he felt those stirrings, wanting to speak her name, to hear her mentioned, no one else must know. Not yet. Not while Kitten was in the way. He'd made a mistake allowing himself to be discussed publicly with Kitten. That wasn't going to happen again.

He said, "I have plans for her. I don't want Kitten exposing her to her cheap friends."

"Les Augustin isn't cheap."

"Who's the other man?"

"I don't know," Mike said. "I never saw him before."

"Some drunken bum she picked up. You tell her I want her to leave Gratia Shawn out of her bouts."

Mike looked at him. "You'd better tell her yourself. Kitten isn't very friendly to suggestions these days."

Mike didn't know. If she had any idea, she wouldn't ask him to speak to Kitten. She didn't know what was between them was beyond grace of words, acts alone remained. He'd fooled her completely. If he could fool Mike, he could fool anyone, including the police. Mike knew him.

The steward had set two other persons across the table. He didn't see their faces, he smiled amiably at their anonymity. "Did you know Kitten Agnew is sitting back there?" He mimicked the middle-aged man's voice. One of these men craned over his shoulder, the other one looked down into his plate. Mike's heel caught his shin. He turned his amiable smile on her. "Good steak," he commented.

Did you know I'm going to kill Kitten Agnew? I had planned it for tonight. The Albuquerque police don't know much. They'd take an accident. They wouldn't doubt Vivien Spender's sad regret. But maybe it's better I'll have to wait until tomorrow night. Maybe it's better that Chicago will have to handle it. Sometimes tanktown cops get pretty officious. They might want to hold all of us for an inquest. Chicago will cooperate. There's movie money there. The real issue will be so confused by the power of money and the industry, by the clutter of attorneys and advisers and officials and flacks and sob sisters, no one will suspect.

Mike said, "Just rare enough."

—2—

Les said, "Don't look now, darling, but the King of the May is behind you."

She controlled the lick of fear that might have curled in her eyes. What difference did it make if Viv were there? It was none of his business now with whom she dined. He was through with her; she was through with him. He couldn't hurt her as long as she was protected by a diner filled with civilized beings.

Hank growled, "Who's the King of the May?"

Kitten lilted sheer laugher. "Darling, who else could it be?"

"Spender." Les explained.

Kitten looked under her eyelids at Les. "I wonder what drove him out among the peasants." It couldn't be because he was stalking her. It wasn't that.

Gratia's voice was kind. "Perhaps he was lonely."

Kitten gurgled. The glance she slanted was as at a country

cousin, a particularly gawky one. "Darling, he's never lonely. He always has Vivien Spender with him. What else could anyone want?" She trilled laughter again, hoping it reached his ears.

Les said, "Quite."

Gratia remained untouched by Kitten's laughter. She sat there watching Hank with her great eyes the way she'd been watching him all through the dinner. As if he were something important to her, as if she were a lovesick school girl worshiping at an unattainable shrine. Kitten's nails clawed the napkin across her lap. Hank wasn't for Gratia. Gratia couldn't hold him for ten minutes; he was a man who'd want meat, not a cold turnip.

Gratia wasn't going to get Hank. She'd thieved Vivien Spender, beyond that she should not trespass. Hank was the first man in years that Kitten had wanted out of emotion, not mind. She had no intention of allowing Gratia to spoil things. Let her have Viv. If she encroached on Hank, she'd regret.

He wasn't paying any attention to the girl. He ate and he drank. Kitten looked at him now with warm eyes. She spoke gaily, "You're eating as if you didn't ever expect to see food again."

At his expression, she drew back. His face had gone suddenly blank and hostile. He ordered, "Shut up."

Les sighed, "Don't start again, Hank."

Hank pushed away his plate. "Let's get out of here. I'm getting sober."

She didn't understand what had happened but she didn't want to leave. Not until after Viv left. She didn't want to pass his table, to meet his eyes, his scheming brain. She refused. "Gratia wants some ice cream. Don't you, Gratia?" She wasn't scoffing at Gratia now; she was Kitten Agnew, the warmhearted American girl.

Gratia shook her head almost in horror. "Oh no." Her eyes whimpered against Hank's face.

Kitten said almost angrily, "Well, I do. And demitasse." She covered her annoyance with a quick moue at Hank. "You don't mind, do you?"

His hostility had gone. He said, "Why not?" She didn't know what had engendered that moment of terrible, unspoken rage. It had passed. But he didn't touch his plate again; he lit a cigarette and gloomed with it.

She and Les ate ice cream. Gratia's melted into a sweet, milky puddle while her eyes watched Hank. Kitten spooned slowly; she couldn't ask if Viv were still there; she didn't dare look over her shoulder. She feared a backwards glance as if she were being pursued.

Yet in spite of the time she consumed, when she rose from the table her eyes met Viv's. He was still in his place a table away. She didn't recognize him, she was able to delay recognition by laughing over her shoulder at whatever Les might have said. Not until she came to his table did she seem to notice him.

Her voice was loud and careless. "Hello, darling! Fancy seeing you in public places." She deliberately blocked the aisle, holding Hank, Les and Gratia penned behind her. They couldn't move until she did; they couldn't leave her with Viv.

Viv hated her. Until this moment she might not have known how permeated he was with hatred of her. It seeped from every pore as he spoke, normally, thinking his disease was hidden. He said, "You'll pardon my not rising, Kitten. I'm wedged."

Hank's hand pushed her shoulder. "Go on, Kitten."

She flung him a smile. "But, darling, I want you to meet Viv. Viv, this is Hank Cavanaugh. Hank, this is Viv Spender." As she spoke her eyes fell carelessly on the man across from Viv. It was the cheap little man from compartment F. His eyes were dog eyes baying up into her face. As she met them, his spoon wavered and consommé dribbled on the starched white tablecloth. She didn't give him recognition, deliberately she turned her back to him.

Viv accepted the introduction as if he were delighted to meet Hank Cavanaugh. Hank didn't. He said brusquely, "Hello. Get on, Kitten."

She didn't move. She was enjoying this. Relishing the warning in Mike's eyes, relishing Viv being relegated to unimportance. Even the disgusting noises Pringle was making over his soup didn't spoil it. She laughed down into Viv's face. "Wonderful trip so far."

Hank had her elbow and was urging her but she didn't move.

"Are you enjoying it, darling, or are you working as usual?"

"Someone has to work," Spender laughed. The laughter was so brittle, a feather's touch would have broken it.

"You'll get dull," Kitten said, and to Hank, "All right, darling!"

She didn't intend to turn her eyes again on Pringle. It was as if she were forced. He was draining the cup of soup. He set it down and he licked the soup from his lips. His tongue licked his salty lips and his eyes lapped her face begging a crumb, one word. She withheld it. She left him gnawing the barren bone of anonymity. She didn't know why he had been put on this train, or why, being aboard, he should continue to dog her steps. She didn't want to be reminded of those who failed to measure up to Spender's demands.

She hurried on out of the car not waiting to hear Viv speak to Gratia. She didn't care what he said, what tonal richness saturated the words. She plunged ahead, wanting only to get away. She forgot Hank; she was alone in the endless moving tunnel. When he spoke behind her, she was startled.

He said, and it was conclusive, "Running away won't help."

—3—

It hadn't been bad, he actually seemed to be enjoying his dinner despite the motley sounds and sights and smells about him. There'd been a touch of the old Viv in his fleeting assumption of the role of the movie-struck traveler, his query to the crumpled man across from him, *Did you know Kitten Agnew is sitting back there?* He had pronounced Kitten's name without a tremor, with unimportance.

Yet Mike did not relax. She knew the moment must come, that Kitten and her party must pass the table on their way out of the diner. She and Viv had entered too late. She saw them rise at last; Viv too saw, his muscles tightened.

She didn't look at Kitten. She saw the shape of the slim gray suit shadowing the table, heard the false merriment of the greeting, *Hello, darling.* Mike couldn't look at Viv, she focused her eyes across the table.

The man across from Viv was bent over a cup of consommé. His mouth was too noisy on the soup, it slapped above train noise, above the painted dialogue of Kitten and Viv Spender. Mike was watching when Kitten's eyes carelessly turned on the man, when his spoon wavered and the stain of consommé spread on the clean white of the cloth. She saw him put down the spoon, debased; she saw something else, that Kitten and this man had known each other somewhere, sometime.

Kitten turned cruelly away from his shame. The man sat there quivering, his nose hungry above the soup. His soiled nails crept to the spoon. Unobtrusively he took it up, supped again. He was hungry, only a hungry man would have denied his pride for a mouthful of liquid.

She recognized now his hesitation over the menu when he had been seated. She hadn't at the time been conscious of why his eyes crept from the printed card to the broiled steak on her plate and on Viv's. She hadn't been conscious of his bitter abnegation when he ordered chicken fricassee; she had considered it a matter of taste. She realized now. Chicken fricassee, one dollar fifty; steak dinner, two fifty.

The man was poor. How did he know Kitten? How did she know him? His eyes were begging recognition of her but she kept her back turned on him. When she moved away, resignation stoned him. He did not lift his hands to protect himself.

Kitten moved on and after her the tall man with the lined face, Hank Cavanaugh. Behind Cavanaugh came Gratia and Viv's smile was pathetically real. "Having a nice trip, Miss Shawn?"

"Very nice." Mike's eyes fastened on the girl. There was something shining beneath the Shawn's pale skin when she smiled. She didn't hesitate, asking Spender's further notice. She was as unlike one of Spender's discoveries as a flesh and blood woman. She went quietly on. Les Augustin followed her, speaking, "Hello, Viv," in passing.

Spender didn't smile, he was forcedly courteous. "Hello, Les."

Spender attacked his ice cream. The four were out of hearing before he spoke. "Who the hell is Hank Cavanaugh?"

Mike said, "He's a newspaperman."

Spender turned his head to her.

She said dryly, "He's not a gossip writer. He writes literature. The kind that tears your guts."

Spender ate again. "Maybe we could hire him."

"Maybe you could," Mike said. She didn't sound promising.

"You might look into it."

It was pure error that her eyes fell upon the pathetic man at that moment. Error because he should have been unseen in his hopelessness. He pushed away his dinner plate. His face was sick with pity as he crept away from the table seeking the small comfort of a hole.

Viv remarked, "He didn't finish his dinner." He eyed the chicken fricassee with distaste. "He should have ordered the steak."

—4—

He said, "You can't run fast enough or far enough."

He closed the door of Les's compartment. She was standing there swaying with the train but it wasn't the motion of rushing wheels that trembled through her. She didn't seem to know when he put her in the Pullman seat, sat down, opposite her. "Spill it," he ordered.

She looked at him then, and he knew she'd lie. The intonation of her laugher was a lie. "What are you talking about?" she asked. "Give me a cigarette, darling."

He didn't give her a cigarette. He said, "I wasn't talking. You must have been listening to clacking in your head."

Her eyes narrowed under her displeasure. But her fingers trembled as she took a cigarette from her giant, expensive suede handbag. "You could give me a light," she said.

"I could if I wanted to," he told her flatly. He kept his hands in his pockets. Anger would strip off her sham. He'd forgotten that Gratia and Les would be following. They entered now and he spoke harshly to them. "Go away and leave us alone."

Les pointedly refused the suggestion. He said, because it was expected of him to say things like that, "What are we doing, choosing up sides?" He came in and sat down beside Kitten.

Gratia stood, hesitant, on the outskirts. Hank couldn't tell her what he would. That he wanted to be with her, alone and in peace. That what he was doing with Kitten was out of a compulsion, stronger than his want; that he must make this attempt to save Kitten in spite of herself. He could tell Gratia nothing. He held silence while in her eyes was the uncertainty of the unwanted. He turned on Les again. "Go away."

"I might point out this is my compartment."

Hank strengthened it, "Go away and be selfish," but Les didn't understand. Les hadn't seen that sudden headlong panic with which Kitten was possessed as she left the diner.

Les's smile invited Gratia. "He's been fed. He won't bite." He toed Hank nearer the window. "Haven't you any manners? Make room for Gratia."

Gratia said, "I'm tired. I think I'll go to bed."

"No." Les's refusal wasn't acting. He was fleet, across the room beside her. "Not yet, darling." Hank wanted to throw Augustin's crawling hand off her arm but he only said savagely, "There's no reason for you to go if Les is staying. He needs someone for company."

Her eyes were on him as they had been throughout dinner. Reproaching him for getting her into this and then deserting her for the tarnished glitter of Kitten. He took it.

She insisted, "I really am tired. Would you mind if I had the room made up, Kitten?"

Les was pulling her gently to the seats. "Don't think about Kitten. It's your room too, isn't it?"

She smiled at Kitten. "I'm just a guest."

Kitten said expansively, "Have it made up whenever you choose." She masked malice in chaff. "Ignore Les. He doesn't care what you do. He's only trying to play a scene. He fancies he's an actor, don't you, sweet?"

"I am an actor." Les's voice was tired. He looked tired, tired in his very veins. They stood thin and blue on his temples, his wrists. "But you're wrong. I do care." Hank saw it in that moment. Les too had found the peace of Gratia. He too feared losing it. He had need of it.

He had led Gratia to the seat and he placed her next to

Hank. "You won't go until you've had a brandy, will you? You can wait that long."

"Just that long," Gratia said. She was careful not to come into contact with even Hank's coat sleeve. She sat quietly in the corner where she was placed. Yet, strangely enough, he was physically conscious of her in every membrane. So strong was the consciousness that there was no sense of touch for him in Kitten's legs stretched out against his.

Les brought the small glass of brandy to Gratia. "To dream on," he said.

Hank's demand was too loud, too determined to destroy the fragile thread winding Gratia to Les. "For God's sake, are we pariahs?"

"Yes," Les smiled. "If you want one, the bottle's there."

Hank saw the maneuver and he laughed with real enjoyment for the moment. Laughed at the little change in Augustin despite the fact that the fellow was straddled on a high star. The same sly way of satisfying his will. Les intended to sit beside Gratia; but he wouldn't request, he'd scheme.

It gave Hank honest if ugly pleasure to thwart him. He leaned back simulating comfort. "Pour us a drink, Kitten."

She was petulant. Beneath the petulance was impotent fury. She was too feminine not to understand the undercover war for Gratia between the two men. She said, "If I have to pour it, I don't want one. You don't need one."

"Hospitality," Hank grunted.

Gratia lifted her eyes to Les. "I don't want to drink alone."

He moved then, gently.

Kitten's words pricked blood. "Darling, this is wonderful! The great Augustin jumps through a hoop."

Les bowed over her glass. "You wouldn't understand," he said. It was more than rebuke. Its very quietness was devastation.

Hank slid his spine upright. Les Augustin, created without

an honest emotion, transfigured. By a woman, a simple, quiet girl. His eyes pried into Les. But it wasn't a pose. Les handed him a drink, held his own glass and sat down opposite Gratia again.

Hank gulped the burning drink, scarcely hearing Les's remonstrance, "It's brandy, my friend." Les wasn't good enough for her; God knew he himself wasn't. The word was good and the word was right. Gratia was good; neither of them was fit to touch her.

Gratia put down her glass. "You don't mind?" she asked, rising. She was ivory and shadow in the poor light.

Les said, "No—darling," The darling didn't come out something brittle. It was sweet on his tongue. He went with her to the door.

Hank watched them across the small box of the room. He didn't answer her spoken, "Good night." She wasn't for him. She wasn't for Les either but Les wouldn't remember her long. There were no deeps in Augustin. Yet Hank was quickly resentful when Les left the room with her.

Kitten mocked, "And that is that."

His hands clenched. He struck at her with his mouth. "Why did you run?"

She flared, "I didn't."

"You did." He was brutal. "You ran because you were afraid. What were you afraid of?" He cursed aloud as Les returned almost at once. "I thought you were going to respect our privacy this time," he said.

Les didn't answer him.

Kitten said, "You were positively mawkish, Augustin. Are you ill?"

"Yes," he said. He poured another thimble of brandy. "I want to go to bed."

"What about us?" Hank demanded.

"I'm not going to bed yet," Les told him. "There's something I have to do first. I won't be long." He swallowed the drink and he went away again. Hank's scowl wondered.

Kitten began, "She looks innocent—"

Hank cut her off sharply. He hammered, "Why are you afraid?"

—5—

He said, "Hello, Mike."

He hadn't knocked or if he had it was lost in the clank and clatter of train sound. He suddenly materialized in her doorway with his languid, "Hello, Mike."

"Hello, Les." She didn't know him well; she didn't know why he was here, only out of presentiment. She was curious and she was wary. She pushed aside the papers on which she had been working, being careful to cover them. His reputation had walked before him. She waited, her eyes alert behind the slant green glasses, as he closed the door and lounged down across from her.

He didn't dawdle. He came at once to the reason for his seeking her. But he asked it idly. "What gives with Kitten?"

She was quick. "You mean that refugee from a lost week-end with whom she's appearing? I thought you could tell me."

She'd not sparred with him before; the flicker in his eyes savored her worth.

"I could." He didn't intend that she be allowed time to think. He struck. "I mean the first Mrs. Spender."

"What about her?"

Just before her eyes went blank, they flecked fear. She hadn't been on guard soon enough. He saw it. He mused, "How did she die?"

She struck back but she was afraid. She demanded, "What's Kitten been saying?"

"Nothing." He put on wings of seraphic innocence. "Nothing at all. I was just wondering."

Mike's voice was tight in her throat. "What have you heard?"

"Nothing, I just wondered, how did she die? An accident?"

Mike said flatly, "It was an accident. She took an overdose of sleeping tablets. I don't think Kitten ought to be talking loosely about it. Viv wouldn't like it." Augustin hadn't known. He hadn't dreamed of its enormity. He was for all his tired worldliness a little fearful of the surface he'd scratched. She was sickened. She'd thought too much on it, now she'd given it away. Not in words spoken, in fear unspoken.

He was smiling under his eyelids. As if he could see her better that way, in perspective. She stiffened against what was to come, afraid to talk of it; afraid to think . . .

He said, "Come, Mike. We know Kitten and Viv are—no longer compatible, should I say?" He was deadly quiet. "Perhaps Kitten wants it widely known she doesn't take sleeping tablets."

It was said. Her color was gone, the rim of her lips was bleached as sulphur. She closed her eyes to her dread reflection, closing out Les Augustin, but he didn't go away. He was there when her eyes opened again wearily. Whatever Viv was, he was hers; she would fight for him. She had always fought for him. She spoke slowly, firmly. "Kitten's made some ugly allegations about Viv. But that one's a little too much."

He shrugged. "What has she said? You're putting words in her mouth, Mike. I'm not."

Her fingers were laced tight as stays. "Why did you come here?"

"Just to pass the time of day, Mike."

She wanted to revile him for carrion; it was in her teeth. But she bit the words back from her lower lip. She was afraid of him. She said, "Kitten sent you."

"Sorry to disillusion you, sweetheart. Kitten is far too busy entertaining Hank Cavanaugh to care where I am or what I'm doing."

She set her lips with thin disgust. "Then you've been scavenging in old gossip scows. I don't know what you want. Nothing from Viv, and there's no reason for you to want to do anything to him. You aren't any knight in shining armor for Kitten. Even if you wanted to be, she could tell you she doesn't need you when she has Seager. You'd better forget it."

"I'll forget it." He was agreeable but he didn't move. He held the pause just long enough. "I don't know about Cavanaugh."

"What do you mean?"

Les opened his thin cigarette case. "Don't you know about Hank? Wonderful fellow. The Augustin of the press." He put the cigarette between his lips. The sharp closing of the case scraped Mike's nerves.

"What are you trying to tell me?" Her mouth was rude.

"I'm talking about my friend, Hank Cavanaugh."

"You needn't. I know his reputation."

"But Mike, my love, you've never seen him in action." He blew smoke idly. "You ought to tell Viv about Hank."

She understood what he inferred. But she forced indignation. "Viv knows about Hank. He'd like to hire him."

Leslie's laughter curled like a thin whip. "Oh, no."

"Not everyone scorns the flesh pots as you do."

"Oh, no," he trickled. "Oh, no, Mike." He was under her skin where he wanted to be. "I don't scorn flesh pots, my sweet. To think you could put that connotation on my rejection of Viv Spender's offers. I who was a starving genius so few years ago. I merely wait for a man of wit. Hardly Spender."

He was deliberately trying for insult. But he meant it. That came as shock, hideous shock. Tears stung hotly behind her eyes. It was thus the younger artists saw Vivien Spender, a man of money-bags, not of artistry. She had known, not that anyone would dare tell her. But she had known in him, known and held her peace, known and refused to know. Her head was bent, her tears withheld. She said, "I wish you'd get out and let me work."

"Mike!" His eyebrows were pained. "This is not the diplomacy of New Essany productions."

"And this isn't New Essany productions. It's my room on the Chief."

He sighed, "I'll go." But again he didn't move. He merely stirred languidly. "First tell me what gives with Kitten? Second, tell me why the first Mrs. Spender who died accidentally is only mentioned accidentally? And lastly"—his eyes hardened beneath his lids—"what grandiose, if brief, plans does Viv have for Gratia Shawn?"

The barricade had been forced down. Because she was weary of the burden that weighted her shoulders alone. Because she wanted the release of talk. Because she wanted to be rid of him and knew this was the only way. But she would tell him only what he knew.

She was businesslike, she might have read from a report. "Kitten is going to take Viv to court if he doesn't let her play Clavdia Chauchat. She'll throw the book at him. She has dates, place names, witnesses. Certain laws were violated, one certain law drafted to protect girls who don't know better, but only used by girls who know too well. Girls like Kitten Agnew. He'll fight, and he won't lose. He doesn't know how to lose. I've tried to warn Kitten to drop it; he's making her a generous offer for release."

"Viv Spender, like his protégée Kitten, hasn't a generous fingernail," he mused.

"Have it your way. Neither of them will give an inch. Maybe you could talk to Kitten. She doesn't hear what I say."

He shrugged. "I don't believe Kitten would refuse a generous offer. If she knows he won't give in on Chauchat, she'll take the money rather than a long-drawn-out suit which she could lose."

Mike stated, "I'm not inventing. Her terms are Clavdia Chauchat or the new Mrs. Spender."

He closed down his eyelids. She had given him titillation. This was delicious shock. But he didn't forget. He slitted a glance. "And secondly—"

She was groping for it.

"The first Mrs. Spender."

She said sharply, "We don't talk about Althea Spender because it's a sad memory for Viv. Even you should realize that."

"Yes. Quite obvious." His smile was insulting. "A sad secret memory." He unfolded himself slowly.

"As for your last question—" she began.

He didn't want it answered. She realized suddenly, with curious surprise. He didn't want Gratia touched by the fixed situation; if she were, he didn't want to know.

Because she feared and hated this man, Mike was relentless. "Viv will star her."

She heard the feather of his sigh. She said harshly, "She'll sleep on plenty of salt pillows before she sees her name in lights. What difference does it make to you?"

It couldn't matter to him, not to Leslie Augustin who'd had every sort of beauty flung at him. It couldn't be he'd gone soft over a girl he'd never seen until this day, a girl beautiful and gentle, yes, but as remote as Betelgeuse. Why then did he stand there, his quips silenced, tonguetied as a lovesick swain? If it had happened, if Gratia had in some fashion bewitched Augustin, she had forged a weapon for Mike's hands. A weapon Mike might need to silence this adder tongue, to guerdon Viv.

"The new Clavdia," she said ironically.

His lips were bitter on the echo line. "The new Clavdia."

—6—

The night was rushing by on fearful black wings. The stars were desert bright, sharp as tiger tooth. The sound of wind and sound of the train lashed at them where they stood outside the dim windows of the observation car. The wind pulled back her Valkyrie hair, lifted her face. In the dark her eyes were dark and her mouth trembled. She flattened herself against him and her body trembled like her mouth.

He didn't touch her. "You want danger."

"No. No." She was whispering above the fury. "I'm afraid."

"Of what?"

When she answered, he heard only by the shape of her lips. "Of death."

She'd broken at last; she had said it. And she was shaken after she'd said it. He put his hands under her elbows, clutched to steady her. He said, "There are worse things."

"Oh, no."

He couldn't make her understand that. She'd not been educated beyond simple words. To her the most bitter cup was to be cut away from life. To lose this amber hair, this crimson mouth, this molten flesh; to receive in its place the cold ash of oblivion.

He repeated, "There're worse things. There's wishing you could die. There's wishing you could close your eyes and your memory forever."

She pressed closer into him. "Forever. What is forever? Do you go on and on—until you can't stand it any longer—and then you go on and on—"

He stopped her sharply. "Don't talk like that. Don't think it. You don't know what's beyond."

"We learned at Sunday School—golden harps and angels—I wish that were it. Marble halls. Nobody believes that now."

He'd thought about it too. When he faced death daily, yearly. He knew now she wasn't inventing her fear. "Nobody's ever known," he said. "It's too big for us. We couldn't be told."

"Heaven," she was talking to herself. Like a child, a frantic child. "I don't believe in heaven. I don't believe in hell. What will happen to me?"

He could only answer her out of his own terrible knowledge. "I believe in hell. I've watched men in hell. Men and women. Even children. I've watched the devils torture them. I watched and I made a lot of money and I won a medal." The hurt was clawing him. She'd made him think about it.

She wasn't listening. "Where will I go? What will happen to me?"

That was all she cared about, what would happen to her. Revulsion pressed up into his throat. He swallowed it. She wasn't any different from anyone else. Me was first with everyone. Why make it out it wasn't?

But she'd made him remember. "Sure I believe in hell. Injustice, that's hell. Uselessness, wanting to do and not being able to, that's hell. Starving—I've watched men starve. And women. And children. Starving because they didn't grow food." Helpless fury sickened him. "I don't know why they didn't grow it; maybe they couldn't, maybe they didn't have a chance. Maybe they didn't want to, weren't smart enough to want to. So they've got to starve because the growers didn't grow the food to feed the hungry. They grew it to trade for *yen*. They'd let it rot before they gave it away. But listen to this, if they gave it away, they'd starve next season. Because they wouldn't have enough *yen* to make more food grow. That's the way it is. All mixed up. That's hell."

Her eyes were fearful and he knew the look she'd seen on his face. "I don't know what you're talking about."

"Famine. In the East."

"I've read about it."

"I wrote about it." Famine and War. War breeding destruction. The Horsemen of Chaos waiting their time. Madness. Hell. Once he hadn't believed in hell. Once he hadn't believed in a personal demoniac deity. But he'd seen men possessed. He knew powers of evil flogged the earth and powers of good weren't strong enough to exorcise them. The powers of good, what had happened to them? Where was heaven? If there was hell, there must be heaven. There must be the balance.

He said bitterly, "We have to die to get to heaven."

She began to tremble again. "I'm afraid to die. I don't want to die."

His harsh laugh startled her. "You don't want to die. I don't want to die. All God's chillun don't want to die. They want to live in hell. That's the joke of it. That's why if you keep quiet you can hear the Devil laughing. Everyone's begging to go on being tortured. But it won't do any good. Eat, drink and be merry for tomorrow you die." He set her away. "The trouble is we're sober, Kitten. We need a drink."

She said sadly, "Everyone's gone to bed. We can't go to my room, Gratia's gone to bed. Les has gone to bed in your room."

He put his arm around her, "I brought a bottle. Sit down and we'll pour a drink. That's the only medicine for the gremlins in the dome." He took Les's brandy bottle from his pocket. "Here you are, baby."

She took a swallow and sat down in the canvas chair.

"That won't drown them. That just tantalizes them." He drank long, took a gulp of air, drank again. The burning was good. He could finish this one and the haze would ripple across memory. He remembered then. He'd brought her out here to find out about her. He put away the bottle. She was sitting there shivering.

He sat down beside her. "Why have you death in your mind?" It didn't belong there. She was on top of the heap. That had come across at dinner.

She looked at him for a long moment. The wind and the darkness and fear had stripped her face. She said, "Viv Spender is going to kill me."

Viv Spender. The name that had upcropped all day, ever since he ran into Les Augustin in the club car after lunch. "He's the big guy you talked to after dinner. You introduced me."

She was pathetically eager to talk now. "He made me. I wasn't anything. He took me out of a dump and he made me a great star. I didn't have anything. Not even looks. He trained me, the way you'd train a dog." She might have been reading lines. "I didn't trust him. I knew what he'd done to other girls he'd discovered and made great—and thrown away. I wasn't going to let that happen to me."

"It hasn't happened."

"It can't happen. I protected myself too well. The only thing he can do is"—she whispered it—"kill me."

To blast her out of it, he scoffed. "Are you always this morbid?"

She spoke between her teeth. "You're like everyone else. You think because he's so important that he wouldn't dare risk it. There won't be any risk. No one will know." He barely caught the whisper. "It will be like the way he killed his wife."

Because he didn't know what to say, he took another drink. She could be nuts. She could be morbid. She could be speaking the truth. "So Spender killed his wife? What did he do that for?"

"It was the only way he could get rid of her."

"And you think he'll do the same to you? Because it's the only way he can get rid of you?"

She nodded dumbly.

"I'd be easier to get rid of, if I were you."

"No." The line of her jaw was stubborn. "I won't let him do to me what he did to the others."

"You'd rather be dead."

"No!" It was sharp. "If I stay out of his way, if I'm with you, he can't kill me, can he?"

"I don't know." He drank again. This was a new approach to the old game. Crazy like a fox, she was. He didn't want her. Liquor was better for forgetting. He'd tried everything; only liquor worked. "Why does he want to get rid of you?"

She said, "Because he's found someone new. Gratia Shawn."

The bottle was empty. Gratia Shawn. He didn't want to move. He didn't want to think. He wanted to close his eyes, to rush with the wind and percussion into oblivion. Gratia Shawn. Because she was good, the powers of evil were stalking her. He should have known. He had known. It was the reason he had refused to let her remain alone this afternoon, unprotected. Her innocence had not beheld the face of evil; she had no knowledge with which to recognize that face. It was why he must protect Kitten the ungood from evil; in protecting her, he would learn the pattern, he would save Gratia Shawn. He closed his eyes.

She said suddenly, "I'm cold."

He opened his eyes slowly, seeing her through their blur. She looked very young huddled there. He put out his hand, touched her blown hair. "Aramantha," he said. *"Aramantha, braid no more that shining hair."*

He didn't know why he'd said that. Something to do with Les, mocking at Les with quotations. A game they'd played. He didn't know how long his eyes had been closed. He only knew the fear had come over her again, she was trembling with it. He pulled her out of the chair.

"You are cold." He took her hand. "Let's go to bed."

FOUR

Deborah Crandall said to Fred Crandall, her husband of exactly twenty-fours hours, "Isn't it a beautiful day?"

He saw her shining face. "Beautiful," he said.

—2—

Mrs. Shellabarger said to Mr. Shellabarger, "Isn't it exciting being on the same train with so many movie people?"

Mr. Shellabarger said, "I never could shave on a train without cutting myself."

—3—

James Cobbett stood on the brick walk in the Albuquerque sunshine. C and E were out early. He hadn't expected C to be up so soon; you wouldn't expect it of honeymooners. They were a happy-looking couple, walking now on the brick walk. Healthy-looking too, as if they played tennis and swam every day. They probably did and the inactivity of the train cramped them. He liked a game of tennis himself. Not that he had much chance at it, but summers between trips he'd get in a few games on the public courts.

He'd expected E to be out at Albuquerque. Old folks didn't sleep so well, usually cranky mornings. The old man acted as if he'd rather be having his coffee than getting this breath of fresh air. They'd want their compartment made up right away.

C and E were all he'd have to do before noon. And maybe F. The sleazy little man in F had been quiet enough yesterday but that didn't mean he'd be that way today. Probably just the opposite, asserting his rights. Anybody as full of wrongs as F would be just as full of rights. He grimaced to himself. Pretty smart, must remember that one for Mary. A wife was a good thing for a man to have; kept you from being lonesome on the road, knowing you were going back to someone who appreciated your foolishment.

He was a little surprised to see the lady in the green glasses coming up the walk. She belonged to Mr. Spender's world, not with the early risers. She came from the Western Union cart; she'd been sending wires. She didn't look as if she'd slept much, beneath the green glasses her eyes were hollow.

His celebrities had been pretty quiet last night on the whole. He'd been surprised to make up Miss Agnew's room early. It wasn't she asked it; it was the other girl, the quiet one. The one who looked like a companion. Miss Agnew and the drunk had left the car when Augustin wanted his compartment made up. That was long before midnight. He hadn't seen them return.

He'd made up Spender's room at midnight but the man's light was on far later than that. Pringle's light had been on late too. He'd had to listen to Pringle while he made up the compartment. The man had stood there in the doorway, calling him Jim, and professing brotherhood. Cobbett didn't want personal brotherhood with Pringle, and no one, not even his wife, called him other than James. He'd been right again on a first view; he'd recognized Pringle for what he was. There was no surprise in Pringle; he followed the age old pattern of a man in the travail of failure. By brothering Cobbett, he abased himself and at the same time raised himself to esteem. This man is lesser than I am; I raise myself by considering him. It would never occur to a Sidney Pringle that a man's pigmentation did not make him a mean creature. That all men were human and as such differed one from another; and as such were the same, one to another.

To Pringle, James Cobbett wasn't a man, he was a mass, a problem. To James Cobbett, Pringle was a man and a man he wouldn't care to invite to his home. Cobbett had pride in himself, he didn't consider a man equal to him unless he were equal in dignity and pride. Mary called him a snob. Well, he'd admit it. He was a snob. It hadn't anything to do with what a man did or what a man possessed; it was what he was. Cobbett was a snob about the I am, He is.

The way I see it, Mary . . . Explaining in the night where the dark made words easy. There wouldn't be any problems of race or religion if you could make men see the I am, He is. You'd take a man on what he was.

And where would the Pringles be in James Cobbett's scheme of things? Well, maybe Pringle wouldn't be such a miserable specimen if he didn't have to compete in worldly ways for his place among men. If you could ease him up, he might turn out to be a nice little fellow. A nice little fellow in a world where a little fellow was just as wanted as a big fellow. The Pringles of the world could all be happy together. They wouldn't have to try to squeeze in where they weren't wanted if they were just as important being small as big. The trouble was that men were always trying to solve problems on an economic, political and emotional basis. Until they utilized reason, nothing would be solved. And sadly, he admitted, you must have rational men to employ reason.

You think too much, Cobbett. Why don't you be like Rufe and the others, live for your wages and the layover? Do your thinking ready-made out of other men's brains and bellies. You won't live long enough to see the age of reason and all its decencies.

The chant riffled down the line. "Bo—ard." The woman in green glasses, Spender's secretary, stepped up into this car. She was out of sight before Cobbett had closed the vestibule trap. He didn't think Mr. Spender would be calling her this early. Probably gone into her own car.

The neat elderly man and his neat gray wife were standing in their compartment, the door open, as he passed. The man said, "Would you make up our compartment, porter? We're going in to breakfast."

He said, "Yes, sir."

Nothing any different from the usual run. Make up E, Mr. and Mrs. Shellabarger of Detroit. Make up Mr. and Mrs. Crandall, they'd got on board up by the diner. Wait around for the others, be afternoon. He came face to face with the girl who shared with Miss Agnew.

He hadn't actually noticed her yesterday. Now he saw the pale heart of her face against the darkness of the room she was leaving. Her eyes meeting his were wide and wondering, as if he'd startled her out of a dream. He himself was startled into saying, "Good morning;" he who had learned to withhold greeting until it was offered.

She said, "Good morning," gravely, sweetly.

This must be the something different he'd been seeking on this run, seeking unconsciously through his reiteration that all was the same. She was the different, a stranger in an alien world. She closed the door of her room and she stood there, outlined against it, unmoving. He saw her beauty then and he wondered at the ways of the white man that this girl should pass unnoticed, that the pattern of desire should be Kitten Agnew.

She spoke again, "Mr. Cobbett."

The name was framed there on the wall, a small measure of dignity. The ones who called him Mr. Cobbett were few. He didn't know her name, she wasn't on the ticket list. He said, "Yes, Miss."

She was hesitant. "Mr. Augustin asked me to breakfast with him this morning. Could you call him for me?"

He smiled. He advised, "You're a little early for these Hollywood folks, Miss. They eat their breakfast about noon."

She returned his smile. "That's what I was afraid of," she admitted. "That's why I didn't want to disturb him." Her smile was confidential. "I'm hungry." She turned and went towards the diner.

James Cobbett went in to make up the Shellabargers' crumpled beds. He felt good. He'd have to tell Mary about this pretty girl. Mary was smarter than he about women. She'd be able to figure out what a girl like that was doing among strangers.

—4—

It had seemed a simple matter last night. Clear, straight-line planning with simplicity as its keynote. He hadn't slept well. The metallic clatter of wheels on rails, the whor of trains counterpassing by night, the hoot of whistle, the ceaseless motion. Together, separately, each banished sleep. He'd been forced to take two sleeping tablets before sleep came; waking now, he resented the drug. His mouth was dry, his eyes heavy, his step sluggish as he walked to the bath for a bromo.

He'd gone to sleep with Kitten irritation scraping his nerves; he woke to the same rasp. If it were not for her threats, he wouldn't have had to undergo this transcontinental trip by train.

If it were not for her, he wouldn't have needed a bromide, nor would he need a bromo now.

It wasn't fury at her that burned in him this morning; it was too early for the engendering of strong emotion. It was the nasty smallness of irritation. He drained the frothing glass and returned to bed.

It was when he closed his eyes hoping for a reprise of sleep, that there arose doubts of his plan. If Kitten was stricken after visiting his drawing room, a finger of suspicion might be leveled at him. Not that anything could be proved; of that he was certain. But a whisper could be as perilous as a scream. To visit Kitten in her own drawing room was out of the question now. Gratia must not figure in this. If it had happened last night there'd have been no question of Gratia having the finger pointed at her. The delay had changed that. Gratia had been seen too much yesterday. She and Kitten were linked.

He'd work it out. He had the day. It would be safe but how he didn't know. It was bad luck that Augustin was in this particular car. The fellow had a reputation as a nosy gossip. And Kitten had been with the man yesterday; no telling how much she'd talked. There was no one else to bother about. An old businessman and his wife, a young fellow and his bride, somebody named Sidney Pringle. The name was faintly familiar and momentarily he tried to place it. It wasn't important. If he'd had Mike check the passenger list before they came on board rather than after, he'd have had Augustin moved. It had never occurred to him. It didn't occur to him now that a look at the list might have been denied him. He had ways of accomplishing the impossible.

He couldn't sleep; the train was making an infernal din. He got out of bed, put on the maraschino tie-satin robe, knotted the black scarf about it and rang. His good smile was on his face when Cobbett tapped.

He said, "Wonder if you could make up that couch while I'm

shaving, Cobbett? Hate to bother you but I'd like to do some work while I'm having breakfast." The great Spender, courteous, pleasant, sure. A man who could pay for special service.

Cobbett said, "No trouble at all, Mr. Spender."

Viv was finished with his shave when the seats clacked into place. He smiled again. "Now if you'd send along a waiter and get word to Miss Dana I want her, I'll not bother you for a while."

"No bother, Mr. Spender."

What was it he'd planned for Cobbett yesterday? Oh yes, a secretary. The absurd idea still pleased him. Mike knew too much; if she added suspicion to knowledge, she'd have to be put to grass.

He felt better already as he lit a cigarette and looked out the window. The train was pulling into some frontier town. He took up the timetable. Las Vegas. Next stop Raton. He'd get a bit of air in Raton. La Junta five o'clock. Dodge City nine-thirty. It should be accomplished after Dodge City. Nothing but small towns then until Kansas City, four in the morning. Even if it were discovered, they wouldn't be put off the Chief at that hour. It would be through to Chicago as he wanted it.

He called, "Come in." It was Mike.

She said, "Morning, Viv. Have a good night?" She sat down, took out her book and poised her pencil.

"I had a rotten night," he answered good-naturedly. He folded the timetable together. "Such an assortment of rackets. Finally got up, took nembutal and managed to go out."

She dropped her pencil, retrieved it slowly.

He put down the timetable beside him. "It seems to take forever to cross Arizona and New Mexico." The train was yet winding through the wasteland.

"Big states," she said.

"If I ever decide to travel by train again, you have my permission to get out an order of restraint." He smiled broadly. "Ready?"

Throw the dust of a few letters in her eyes before getting down to the business at hand. He began to dictate; it was mechanics, no necessity to keep his mind on the words his tongue spoke. He didn't even hear the rap on the door until she lifted her eyes towards the sound.

"That'll be the waiter," he remembered. "I'm still fasting." He called out and the small studious man entered, his whites glistening with starch.

Viv gave his pleasant good morning. Mike said dryly, "It's afternoon."

"Don't reprimand," he smiled. Those who remembered him this day would remember an important man who took time for pleasantries and pleasantness. A great man who hadn't forgotten how to be a normal human being. He gave his order, asked, "How about lunch for you, Mike?"

"I had breakfast too late. I'll lunch later."

He raised his eyes to the silent waiter. "You might make that coffee a big pot and bring an extra cup. She's an addict."

"Yes, sir."

The door was but half-closed when he asked, "Where was I now?" He dictated until breakfast was brought in.

She interrupted only once. "I've already wired Silverman about that. From Albuquerque."

He poured coffee for her, indicated it. She came from the chair to sit opposite him. He relaxed at the breakfast table. She didn't know that even his relaxation was a minute part of the mosaic he was assembling.

"You were up early," he commented.

"I went to bed early."

He spoke with his mouth full. "What about that—what's his name, the newspaperman with Kitten at dinner?"

"No chance to see him yet. Kitten had him tied up last night."

"I want to see Kitten today." He let a faint scowl touch his forehead. Erased it with another forkful of omelette. "I want to get this thing settled before we reach New York."

A good night's sleep hadn't banished the Cassandra in Mike. "And if she doesn't settle?"

"She will."

Mike didn't press it; he'd expected more argument but she was quiet. He wanted talk about it now; she must know how rational he'd become about it.

"She's not a fool. My offer's generous."

"It's generous all right," Mike agreed.

"I've been thinking it over, Mike. That suit she's threatened, it can't be any more than a bluff. It would pull her down with me. I don't believe she'd want the pillars to crumble on her, do you?"

"Certainly not." Mike was less apathetic now. Her eye was alive again.

"There wouldn't be a studio that would touch her with a ten-foot pole, now or in the future, if she went into court. She'd be committing suicide. And she's not the suicidal type."

"Definitely not," Mike agreed.

"It's a brazen bluff and I'm calling it Make an appointment with her."

"What time?"

Nine-thirty Dodge City. He gave pretense of considering. "After dinner. Her humor will be less foul." He passed to the next matter. "And see if you can get that what's his name."

"Hank Cavanaugh."

"See if you can get hold of him. Separately."

She finished her coffee. "Anything else?"

Gratia Shawn. He wanted to see Gratia Shawn, the itch to look upon her, to hear her voice was tenfold increased over last night. He must not. He must not be coupled with her in any way until it was over.

"That's all," he said. "Thanks, Mike."

She went out wondering. She could have been wrong. He was himself this morning, no destroying anger, no posturing of insulted ego. She couldn't remember if she'd been wrong about him before. There was a first time for everything. The confinement of the train might have been his only ailment yesterday. The rest her own fantastic fear.

She rapped at Kitten's door in passing. If Kitten weren't awake by now, she ought to be. She'd be prowling all night if she slept all day. There was some response and Mike entered.

Kitten was still in bed, but she'd been out of it some time this morning. Her eyelashes and her hair were brushed, her mouth was painted. Mike wasn't the one whom Kitten expected. The amber eyes were rude. "What do you want?"

Again Mike wondered why she'd wasted time yesterday worrying about this unpleasant little slut. Whatever Kitten received, she deserved. But not death. Even now, looking down at the white satin V that didn't conceal Kitten's breasts, seeing the red-tipped talons, smelling the esoteric perfume, disdaining Kitten and all that which she flaunted, the echo sounded. *But not death.*

Mike said, "Viv wants to see you."

"What for?"

Kitten wouldn't let it be easy, civilized. Mike spoke carefully. "About your contract. He's offering you a million to settle."

Kitten's lips curved away from her teeth. "Isn't that too, too divine?" Her nails curved in until they touched the palms of her hand. "Tell him to go soak his head."

"Now, Kitten." She had the outward form of patience. She'd been forced to the humoring of temperament for so many years. A part of her job. "You should talk it over with him. How about after dinner tonight?"

"I won't see him." She spit out the words.

On Mike's lips was the question, "Why not?" But her tongue was silent. She couldn't ask it; she knew the answer. Her own fears rushed in again. He could have been deliberately misleading her this morning. She above all knew how he could fit a part to himself. At heart he had always been an actor. Perhaps he knew her as well as she knew him. If he had realized what had come into her mind yesterday, he would set out to dispel her suspicions. She didn't ask the question. She said, "Surely you can spare a few minutes."

"Not for him. If you're afraid to tell him to go soak his head, tell him I've gone shopping. Tell him anything. Except that I'll see him. Because I won't." She turned her shoulder on the pillow and closed her eyes.

Mike held her anger. Partly because she was conditioned to insolence from the Kittens of the studio, partly because the fears rode her. She couldn't urge that Kitten change her mind, she was afraid for her to change it. She wouldn't be party to the horror which might come.

She went back to Viv's room. Not so much to report the refusal as to look upon him again, to look into him. He was still seated behind the breakfast table and his eyebrows lifted question.

She said, "Kitten says she can't see you. Her program's full up."

She watched him closely, watched the anger rise in his gorge. The hairs on her head pricked. The anger wasn't unleashed. But his eyes were stones as he smiled, "Thank you, Mike."

Because the wish to save him was desperate, she began, "She won't accept the terms, Viv."

He repeated, "Thank you, Mike."

Kitten had been wrong to refuse. Refusal had roused again that terrible anger. Mike went quickly. She started to her car but she didn't want to be alone with thought now. There was yet the other hopeless errand. It was her job, no matter how foredoomed. She went to the door marked D.

Augustin said, "It's you." He was stretched out on his berth but he was dressed. His casualness ignored their parting last night.

She too could ignore. She mock sighed, "I'm popular today. Mercury where Venus is awaited. Or Apollo. Not that Hank Cavanaugh is an Apollo. Where is he?"

"Haven't an idea." Nor did he care. "He disappeared after dinner last night. Why don't you look in on Kitten?"

"I have. Where's his room?" She wasn't returning to Kitten if she never found Cavanaugh.

"Hasn't one. An upper somewhere. He was going to join me but he didn't." He lifted his eyelids. "Where's Gratia?"

She answered as if he were still casual. "I haven't seen her."

"Not up yet?"

"She's probably been up for hours." She corroborated it. "Kitten's alone. If you see Hank, have him drop in on me. You know where I am."

"She's not with Viv Spender?"

Their eyes met. She said, "Viv's alone too."

His eyes weren't lazy; they were as cold and unmoving as Viv's had been. But he said mildly, "I'd better find Gratia. We're having breakfast together."

—5—

She'd invited him to come this morning. For breakfast. She expected him to come. It was after noon now but she was still expecting him. He'd hardly be up early; the way he'd been drinking last night, he'd lie abed late. But he'd come. She would wait for him.

She wasn't hungry. She had forgotten what it was to be hungry. Yet she could remember when she'd been broke, standing outside bakery windows more than once trembling at the smell of bread stuffs inside. She'd never been able to stand the smell of bread since. Once she'd had the money to buy anything she wanted, she hadn't been hungry any more. The years of scant food had conditioned her to be satisfied with little. Or she'd ruined her stomach not eating. It didn't matter. She didn't have to worry about her weight as did some stars, because she didn't eat enough to put it on.

Last night—she didn't want to remember last night. She'd been a driveling fool. No wonder Hank Cavanaugh had played Old Dog Tray and nothing more. He'd set her down at her door as if she were a sweet sixteen and he the village bumpkin. She'd blown her lines on that one in fine style. A man who'd been billed as the protector wouldn't suddenly become a bedroom invader. It was Gratia's fault, going to bed at sundown. And Les Augustin, Les of all people insisting he was sleepy and intended to go to bed. She ought to demand that Mike Dana find other space for Gratia. Mike could take the girl in; she had a compartment to herself. One thing certain, Gratia wouldn't come barging back in here soon. She couldn't read her damn book in a darkened drawing room.

Mike was turning into a filthy snoop. Bursting in here instead of waiting until Kitten was up and dressed. She wished Hank had been in here. She'd like Mike to take that back to the boss. Viv must think she was a fool if she'd shut herself up with him at any time on this journey. If he had anything to talk over with her, he could do it with Mike. The way he'd been doing for months. She'd had to adopt any number of ruses to get in to see him privately the day she'd given him her ultimatum. This sudden urge to see her wasn't healthy. Perhaps he didn't know she'd read the memorandum Mike had typed. But then, it could have been his own idea, to have Mike show it to her accidentally—on purpose.

She yawned and she turned to the wall, closing her eyes.

She'd be asleep again if Hank didn't hurry up. A waste of hair-dress and makeup if she went back to sleep. She might not hear him knock. That wouldn't keep him out; he wasn't that young. She curled herself comfortably. Hank had forgotten his interest in Gratia quickly enough once Kitten had her hands on him; no he wasn't young.

The rap was small but she heard it and the smile licked her lips. She called out sleepily, "Come in." She didn't turn until she heard the door close, then she rolled over slowly, sleepily, stretch-ing out one arm, opening her eyes slantly.

Her eyes stretched wide. She raised up and she pushed back against the berth wall, her backbone rigid. Her voice was distort-ed crazily. "What are you doing here?"

He stood there in that awful red-pink robe of his, his hands thrust deep into the pockets. For the first time in her life she wanted to scream to keep on screaming. The tiny upcurve of his lips, the treacherous softness of his speech had paralyzed her throat. When she could make sound, she whispered, "You get out of here. Get out of here."

He didn't move. He could kill her now, no one could stop him. They were alone. He mocked. "Are you afraid I'll compro-mise your good name?"

"Get out." She said it mechanically, over and again. "Get out. Get out. Get out—"

"Don't worry. No one saw me come in. Everyone's gone to lunch."

Her eyes stiffened in their sockets. If there were no one in the car, he could carry out his plans. It wasn't just something she thought about; it was actuality. She couldn't speak, her mouth was filled with dust.

His lips were thin. "I dropped in to ask you to cancel one of your appointments. I didn't take Mike's word for it that you were too busy to see me."

Her muscles twitched under the covers.

"I won't keep you long. It is, you realize, purely a business matter."

She opened her parched mouth but no words came from it.

"Shall we say after dinner? Only for a few minutes?"

She said, "Get out." The words were dusty.

Was he going away? His hand was on the knob of the door. She said "No," but he didn't hear it.

"I'll expect you. About nine." He dazzled a smile on her. "You look very beautiful this morning." If he touched her she would die. He didn't touch her.

The door was blank and empty. She was afraid to move. And then she rushed, clipped the bolt and stood there shivering with cold that wasn't in the room. She was not safe alone, not even behind this locked door. She began to dress with frantic, fumbling fingers. She mustn't be alone again.

She wouldn't see him. He couldn't force her to come to him. But she knew his strength, his demands that must be answered. Unless she came to him, he would appear again, unwanted, unannounced. Better to have it over with.

She'd go but not alone. She'd take someone. Mike. Because Mike knew, because if anything happened to her, there'd be someone to make him pay.

And not at night. Anything could happen at night, in the dark. She'd go this afternoon. At the cocktail hour when there was activity in the cars, the club car waiters on the move. When everyone was awake and alert.

"Oh God." She whispered it aloud. It wasn't prayer but it was as near as she could come to prayer after years of neglect. She didn't want to die. She was afraid to go out into the vast unknown stretch of eternity.

She began to dress quickly with trembling fingers. Only long practice in dressing always for admiration gave to the result its practiced finish; another woman would have come out slipshod. She was so cold when she was complete that she caught up the mammoth ruby and pinned it on her breast to warm her. Red for warmth. It wasn't until she fumbled with the catch that she remembered it was his gift. She left it there as a blazing defiance, and as a finger to point. If anything happened to her, it would speak his name.

Her hand touched the knob of the door but it took strength to open it. More strength than in her craven fingers. Blindly she forced it open. He wasn't outside. She stepped out into the corridor, fearing to look behind her to his door, yet fearing to move forward with him possibly at her back.

She saw then, ahead of her, her reprieve. The pudgy man in the crumpled suit, more crumpled this morning, as if he'd tried to press it under a tossing mattress.

She called out, "Good morning."

He barely hesitated; he didn't turn.

She called again, "Good morning, there."

He peered over his shoulder. He didn't believe she was speaking to him, his eyes sought the corridor for some other person. She took quick steps to catch up to him.

He said humbly, "Good morning, Miss Agnew."

He'd shaved this morning but the shadow was already across his jowls; he'd washed his face but it was as pale and gray as if he'd washed in soot.

She swallowed revulsion and she hated Viv Spender for forcing her to accept this miserable oaf for her protection. Sidney Pringle would accept the duty; he was eyeing her now with full realization of her importance, of the dust of it that would cling to him if he appeared publicly in her company.

She was gay. "It's really afternoon, isn't it? You're a late sleeper too, Mr. Pringle."

"I slept late today," he said. "This will be my breakfast."

"Mine too."

He didn't know whether to precede her or to follow her; obviously he'd never walked with a woman through a train. He didn't know about women like her, only of cheap if virtuous girls in hallways. He'd never known a beautiful girl, he'd never known an expensive girl. Her nails and her mouth were stained blood red, her skin was golden and she smelled of perfume. The black satin curved as she walked. She watched the way his chin trembled as he opened the door for her. Watched and despised him. She went ahead of him and she waited at the next door for him to open it. She would rid herself of him as soon as she came upon someone else. They passed through two cars to the club car. She smiled to right and left as she passed through. She carried her head like a lady and her body like a snake. She wasn't any more a lady than her follower was a gentleman but she'd learned. There was no familiar face in any car. Together they entered the diner.

The steward said, "Two? This way."

Her smile over her shoulder was friendly. "You don't mind?" She didn't have to carry him further but she couldn't be sure. Viv Spender might be following. She couldn't chance his intrusion.

The dapper steward drew out her chair at a table for two. Sidney Pringle seated himself.

"You don't mind?" she repeated when the steward left them. "I'm always afraid to correct an authority for fear they'll be cross."

Pringle smiled, "I'm pleased, Miss Agnew," But he wasn't. His eyes were clammy. Looking across at him, at his cheap clothes, she understood why. He didn't have the money to pay for breakfast with Kitten Agnew. Nausea trembled her. Not in years had she been forced to endure this humiliation. Again he was warning of being dropped back into struggle for basic existence. Because of the sick hatred he engendered, she was cruel.

She requested specials not on the menu. He did not look at her, his eyes were on the price list. He ordered the spaghetti lunch, the cheapest and most filling item.

She smiled, "You eat a hearty breakfast."

He was shamed. He tried to carry it off, "Then I won't have to waste time on dinner." He was shamed that she thought him a pig eater. He didn't know that she knew a man ate starchy food because it was cheap.

"That's like an artist," she mocked. "I've always wished I were an artist instead of a craftsman." It pleased him; he didn't sense the mockery. He was too eager for a pat on the head.

She went on, "Hank Cavanaugh says you wrote a wonderful book. Do you know Hank Cavanaugh?"

His eyes were fanned with hope, "I know him through his work."

"He's on board." Her own eyes were restless. She watched the door over his shoulder, as if by talking of Hank, she could conjure his presence. "Maybe you've seen him. A tall, ugly man. But he's brilliant." She looked scornfully into Pringle's eyes. "You should meet him. Fellow admirers."

The waiter laid food in front of them. Sidney Pringle ate hungrily. She forked hers, barely tasting. Because she must keep this man with her until she was with the safety of friends she added, "If we can find him after lunch, I'll introduce you. Would you like to meet him?"

His eyes thanked her soulfully. He couldn't do more than nod, his mouth was filled. He wiped red sauce from his mouth. It stained the napkin. She lidded her eyes to his grossness. The poor were gross because the poor were hungry, the poor were always hungry. He'd doubtless been sitting all morning in a vacuum of hunger, waiting in order that this lunch might serve his stomach for the day. No breakfast; an early heavy lunch, cheaper than dinner. Stay his dinner hunger with peanuts and chocolate bars and apples as polished as wax fruit and as tasteless, sold at the various railroad platforms. Go to bed early, to succulent dreams. She knew because she too had suffered hunger. He didn't know she knew the tricks. He didn't know her loathing of him was because he was forcing her to remember.

To keep from thinking, she asked, "Why are you going east?" It was a stupid question remembering last night. He was going east because he'd failed.

He didn't snivel now. He tried to erase the memory of his weakness by irony. He didn't know his clown face could express only the ludicrous. "I didn't fit in Hollywood," he said.

"Nonsense." She laughed. "What are you going to do in the east?"

He said, "Sell neckties." Behind his smile was bitterness, the arid bitterness of failure.

She had no pity for him. She didn't care if he sold neckties; she didn't care what happened to him. All she wanted from him was safe conduct to Hank Cavanaugh. She didn't want to hear any more of his plans. Because she could silence him by playing the part of Kitten Agnew, the lovable American girl, she asked, "Have you ever tried radio? I've some good friends in it. If you'd like I'll give you their names."

"That's very nice of you, Miss Agnew."

Dear, kind Miss Agnew. If he hounded her, she'd give him names. Let the names worry about getting rid of him.

His eyes moistened. "I've always been interested in radio." She watched the wheels of his mind revolve. Radio paid high money. So many success stories in Hollywood stemmed from radio. He might return in a drawing room with his pick of contracts. Sidney Pringle, writer and producer of that great program . . . "I don't know how to thank you."

"Maybe I'll need a job someday," she laughed and her eyes leaped to the doorway.

Seeing her eyes, he swallowed whole the piece of bread in his mouth. Hope bubbled from him. Hope it was someone important. It was Mike Dana. She came alongside the table. Kitten spoke gayly, "Hello, Mike."

Mike didn't want to stop. Her smile was thin as onion skin, beneath it was the bulwark of her knowledge that Kitten was through. Kitten held her, saying, "Mike, have you met Sidney Pringle? The writer."

He fumbled to his feet. Mike Dana said, "How d' you do, Mr. Pringle." He searched hopelessly for recognition of his name in her face. He found none.

Kitten said, "By the way, he is in a state. He dropped by to insist I see him. I agreed. But I want everything in black and white. Will you go along, Mike?"

Pringle balanced there in the sparse space between table and chair. He tried to look as if he understood the pretense between the women, cloaked in matter-of-factness. There was a drop of red sauce on his chin.

"What time, Kitten?"

She was arrogant. "He said after dinner but I can't make it then. I'll drop in for you. About five."

"Okay, Kitten."

He squeezed down again as Mike passed.

Kitten said, "If you want anything at New Essany, get on to Mike. She's practically the boss."

"I'll remember that," he said humbly. The information was given too late. But he had no time for recriminations, the steward was handing him the check.

Pringle received it and he laid it down on the table while he wiped his damp palms on his napkin. Deliberately she let him suffer while he mawled the napkin, while he counted in his mind the cost of breakfast with Kitten Agnew, the deprivations he must suffer for this. She had no intention of being humiliated by his reluctant money, his meager tip. She waited just long enough before her hand reached across and lifted the check.

He protested, not wanting to protest, "You can't do that. It's been a pleasure eating with you."

She said, "This is on Viv Spender. All expenses paid." She wasn't being kind. She was hard as nails as she signed the check. Viv had forced this companion on her, let Viv pay.

She walked ahead of him but she knew he followed, out of the diner, through the club car, through the Pullman, into their own car. She passed her door. When he stopped at his, she demanded, "Don't you want to meet Hank?" Belatedly she remembered her pleasant smile.

He stammered, "Why, yes." He didn't understand her holding to his company; she didn't care. Again he followed, waiting while she rapped at the door of D, waiting until she opened and closed it, reporting, "Nobody home."

He followed close, past Viv's door, through other cars until she saw them ahead. Cavanaugh, Leslie Augustin, Gratia Shawn. Gratia with her eyes glued on Hank Cavanaugh in the same revolting fashion of last night.

It was Les who first saw Kitten. He said, "Company, children." Gratia's eyes lifted, Hank turned.

They didn't want her to intrude. She didn't care what they wanted. She cried out gayly, "I found you at last!"

—**6**—

He had waked at ten o'clock. He struggled against waking but it did no good; it was inevitable he must open his eyes to rebirth, to another day of pain. His mouth had an ugly taste. His eyes in the small mirror were netted with blood vessels, the grooves about his mouth had worn deeper. He pulled on his trousers, halfway buttoned his shirt, took his kit and descended the ladder. Most of the Pullman was up, neat in dress, disdainful of eye. He felt like a leper as he went down the aisle to the men's room. He should have stayed with Les last night. Why hadn't he?

It was that girl, Kitten. He was afraid she'd follow him to Les's room. He'd come back here so she couldn't find him. He scrubbed his teeth. She'd asked him to come to her room for breakfast, fat chance. He'd said he'd come, anything to get her off his hands last night. He didn't eat breakfast.

The idea of food this early brought revulsion. Her other ideas were worse. In the same breath she talked death and creation. He wasn't interested in her problem. He must have been drunk to get het about it last night. It was that damn Augustin. What did he care now about putting Augustin in his place? Now that Augustin was surnamed the great, his offensiveness was gone.

There was another girl somewhere, a girl with a face that was innocence. A girl who had the promise of peace in her quiet voice. He had found her. He had meant to hang on to her but he'd been out-maneuvered between Kitten and Augustin. He'd take that girl to breakfast. He remembered as he scraped at his chin; he couldn't get to Gratia Shawn without also getting to Kitten. They were in the same room.

When he was dressed, he went along to the club car. He needed a drink. And again he found Gratia. She was sitting there in a chair, reading the small green book. Last night was last night and she might not want to know him today. But he spoke. He spoke awkwardly as a colt, "Hello, there."

She raised her eyes and when she saw him she smiled. Her smile was even lovelier by sober day than by night. She said, "Hello."

There was an unoccupied chair beside her and he sat down in it. "Had breakfast?"

"Long ago," she answered. "Have you?"

"I'm going to. If I can ever catch that rascal's eye."

She looked a little sorry. "Not so early."

He said, "If I had some dark glasses you'd never notice." He ordered a straight one, swallowed its burning brand, left the water untouched. If she hadn't been here beside him, he would have had another. But he was somehow ashamed to in the face of her goodness.

He said, "If you really want to save me from a place on the barroom floor, let's get out of this saloon. I don't know why you're sitting here anyway."

She folded her book together. "I don't want to disturb Kitten. She sleeps late."

"We'll go back to my place. Not so private but we won't be bothered by anyone but strangers." He hurried her because he was afraid Les might come along and spoil things. Or Kitten.

He hadn't yet seen who shared his section. There was a man's briefcase and topcoat laid on the seat but no man. Must have a friend with better accommodations. Hank put Gratia by the window; he sat beside her. He said, "I wanted to talk to you last night but something happened."

"Yes, something happened."

He'd meant to make a speech, to tell her she was something he'd forgotten existed, to doubt that she hadn't been created for his protracted despair. He didn't need the words. She understood there was something between them. She was neither coy nor bold, simply, she understood.

He was chastened. "How long will you be in New York?"

"About two weeks."

"And then?"

"I go back to Hollywood. To start work."

"Do you want to be a movie star?"

She laughed. "You asked me that yesterday. Of course I do. Aren't we always all of us looking for a chance to be in a fairy story? That's what daydreaming is." She said, "I've always day-dreamed."

"Of being a movie star?"

"Never of that." Her eyes were wondrous large, the lashes like delicate fans.

"Of what?"

She protested, "You're persistent, Mr. Cavanaugh. That's because you're a newspaperman. Isn't it?"

He was agreeable. "That's because I'm a newspaperman, Miss Shawn. For God's sake, I was Hank last night. Of what?"

She was slightly embarrassed. "The usual thing, I guess. A handsome prince and a magnificent palace."

"Marriage and money. The usual girlish dream," he grimaced. "Then why the movie angle?"

She lifted her eyebrows. "Don't you see, that's the fairy tale part of it? Receiving what you wouldn't have dreamed of dreaming. And it wasn't as crass as you make it sound." She was hurt rather than angry. "He didn't have to be a millionaire." Her cheeks flushed. "Just—love. Although it sounds silly. Only you can dream that he'll be able to give you everything along with love." Her mouth twisted. "You've mixed me all up. And made me sound like an idiot. What were your dreams?"

"The usual, too," he shrugged. "Fame and fortune. Writing that really great novel. Like the one you're reading."

"You already have part of it, haven't you? Fame—"

"No, lady. No fortune. No fame. I'm going to write a book but it won't be great. It'll make me some money, maybe, maybe not."

She stated, "What you've written has been important. For peace." She was speaking slowly, "You don't know. Maybe your dream has come true more than you know. Maybe when you get to New York you'll find you have fame and fortune, and you will write the great book."

"Maybe not." His smile was crooked.

"Or it might be like me. Your own dream hasn't come true yet but you've been given another one first."

"You think this Hollywood venture is going to bring you your pretty prince and his golden spoon?"

She shook her head. "You don't believe in dreams. Yes, I think so."

He thought of Kitten and he wondered how long before Gratia would be gutted too. That is what fame and fortune did. Only you didn't need them to empty you of spirit. Other things were as effective. The knowledge of your own family in the scheme of things did it just as well. Man had destroyed man, not only in his body but in his soul. Man was no longer large enough to defy. He was a monotonous tick-tack in a cosmic assembly line. He had forgotten that Good was an absolute. He believed in evil and not evil, but he no longer had knowledge of Good.

Her voice was quiet. "A new dream?"

He looked at her, looked long at her. He said, "You're beautiful."

The color was a wave across her face. "You kept saying that last night. As if I weren't real. I am real. And I'm not beautiful, not the way you say it, not the way Kitten is and all those beautiful girls. You know I'm not. Why do you keep saying that?"

He thought out loud. "You are beautiful because you are innocent. You aren't mean or evil or greedy. You don't want to hurt anyone. You don't believe anyone would hurt you. You aren't real. You're part of a dream and the dream is good. God help you when you wake up."

He had disturbed her and regret ate into him. Because he could be wrong. She had walked thus far in a mixed world and her garments were yet as snow. He wanted to explain but how could he explain to her? How could he keep her from waking up, protect her from evil? He was no knight in shining armor; he wasn't the prince she was awaiting. He hadn't a thing to offer her except the gall of his despair.

He saw Leslie Augustin then, coming towards them up the aisle. He was as resentful of the intrusion as if he were young again, and Les a rival for her heart.

Les complained, "I don't know why you wanted to hide." He dropped down into the place of the unknown man.

"We're exclusive," Hank grunted.

Les was looking at her. Hank knew what was behind Les's false face because he himself kept a mask over his own emotions in her presence. He knew that Les felt the same as he about Gratia Shawn. He cherished her. Hank knew his own heart then; knew that cynicism had failed. He wanted to take this girl as his own, forever. He knew as well the idiocy of such an idea. He was too old, too tired, too spattered for that dream.

She said to Les, "I went to breakfast without you. I was too hungry to wait."

"And I kept waiting for you to give me a signal."

Her face was happy turned to Les. But Les Augustin couldn't be the long-awaited prince. He looked like one; he could give her the marble palace, but not the true heart she expected. He was shopworn.

Hank said, "You can't expect a lady to wait till you get up, Augustin."

"And what happened to you last night?"

"I passed out. In my own upper. We might repair to your suite now and have a drink."

Les said, "I don't want to." He caught Hank with his eyes. They weren't light and lazy; they were trying to give meaning without words.

The memory of Kitten's terror on the platform last night split into Hank's brain. He asked quietly, "Anything happened?"

Les shook his head. "Nothing. Yet."

Gratia's mouth was puzzled. "What are you talking about?" There was concern on her brow. "Is it Kitten—"

"Kitten was in bed at noon. Mike told me when she came in looking for Hank."

Hank demanded, "Who's Mike and why me?"

"Mike is Viv Spender's secretary as I told you last night. Spender requests audience with you. I presume he wants to make you a lordly offer."

Gratia asked, "You mean to write for New Essany?" She lifted her eyes hopefully to Hank.

He said, "No thanks," and to her, "That's not in my dream. I'm sticking to the original."

Leslie complained, "Now I'm out of it."

Hank said, "We've been trading daydreams. I've tried to tell Gratia they don't work."

"They don't," Leslie said. "So we make out with second bests."

She said, "Neither of you have any faith. If you believe, it'll come true."

Hank turned again to look on her face. "That's it, isn't it? Your secret. You believe in your dream and nothing you don't want there can get into it."

"I hadn't thought about it." She did now, solemnly. "Perhaps you're right. I won't let anything in that doesn't belong there."

Les asked, "What do you do when you're hungry?"

"She's never been hungry," Hank told him. "If she were, she wouldn't think about it. Because hunger doesn't have a place in the dream."

She pleaded, "I wish you'd stop discussing me. You're both too smart for me. You make me feel that high and stuffed with sawdust."

Les shoved the unknown man's topcoat aside for more comfort. "You don't appreciate your protectors. I'd already nominated myself for that position. Now I'll have to share with Hank. Quite obviously he has the same idea."

She shook her head. "You see? You think I need protection."

"I think you might," Les said gravely.

"I'm not a baby. How do you think I've managed so far without protectors?"

His lips curved. "I think you've always had someone on the job."

Their sham battle was diversion. Hank, remaining outside it, could wonder at the overnight change in Les. It wasn't like Les to be serious; Gratia had done this to him, Gratia and the imminence of Kitten's fear fulfilled. They shouldn't be sitting here dallying; they should be looking out for Kitten. He'd been wrong last night. Gratia could look out for herself; however unworldly she appeared, that very quality was her protection. It was Kitten with all her brazen world wisdom who was helpless. What was stalking Kitten wasn't of the world. It had nothing to do with law and the norm. It was of the spirit. The spirit of evil. The spirit of evil which had dominance in this generation because good was lost.

And Kitten knew. She tried not to know. She clanged brass armor about her; she meshed her eyes from vision of truth. Yet the truth like fog, insinuated. She was shaken with the terror of knowledge of evil. He had seen her shaken.

He didn't care what happened to Kitten but he had to care. Because much as he'd tried to throttle it pity for the hunted, for the weak, for the pitiable, was cancerous in him. Even for Kitten, he must be eaten with pity. Kitten with all her silly vanities, her misshapen pride, her mind hung with foolish baubles, Kitten whom he despised, he must love in pity. Only if he could save her, would he be free of the sore.

There were so few of those marked down as evil's own that he had been able to save. He could not let her pass if by his efforts he could save her. Her fate was personal, the fate of those from whom he had fled was cruelly impersonal. But reduced to the ultimate they were but one to the destroyer. Murder was murder whether it be of one or of many. Murder was the essence of evil; it must be prevented when it could be prevented. He betrayed the many to evil if he did not help the one.

He was about to speak when he saw Kitten coming towards them. So much for brave thoughts. She was sleek black satin, the pin between her breasts was a mammoth ruby that would have bought food for a village of starving Chinese, her radiance was shocking.

She cried out gayly, "I found you at last!"

—7—

After Kitten found them, Hank insisted on returning to Les's space. "We can't smoke here and God knows we can't drink. Let's go where it's civilized." He seized on Kitten as if he'd been starved for the touch of her. She was whole, unbroken. He didn't deserve she should be; he had fled her last night, had furthered his desertion this morning. She should be dead now, her blood upon him for his omission. In a world ruled by geometric precision, her fear of death would have been consummated in death.

It was nothing to him if she died; she was nothing to him. He was not his sister's keeper; violently he rejected the load. Yet it had been placed on him not once but again. He could not let her die, not if it was within his power to save her. He had been powerless to save the many. Being powerless, he had turned craven, he had run away. He was not cowardly enough to run again.

Les agreed reluctantly to the move. "If you insist." His hand sighed out to Gratia. "He insists." Les could not save Kitten. He hadn't the strength, physical or moral. Les didn't care what happened to her. He had curiosity but no sorrow in his heart.

Gratia was colored by Les's reluctance to leave here. Hank avoided her face. He didn't want to know if it was with her as it was with him. That their coming together was important, that it held secret meaning and hope of eventual translation of the secret. He didn't want to know if there was hidden beggary on her face as there could have been on his. If her reluctance was because she clung to a dream that these others would go away leaving Hank and her fumbling again towards each other.

He was a fool. She was gentle and gracious with him because these qualities were of her nature. She was the same with Les. By her very simplicity, she would be aware of values. She knew this was chance encounter, that when the Chief ended its run, each person aboard would return to his own separate self. This was more brief than summer romance; this was journey, the meeting and the parting almost one. The romance was in his heart alone.

Kitten was eager, nuzzling the sway of her black satin body against Hank. He demanded harshly, "What are we waiting for?" and he turned abruptly, shutting out Gratia by the finality of his back.

The shapeless lump of man who had been with Kitten was in the way. He wasn't with her any more; he was standing on the outskirts, begging with his watery brown eyes. Hank said, "Come along," to him as he shoved past. He didn't know who the man was nor why he should include him. Kitten didn't like his saying it, her frown was dark. She echoed, "Yes, do come along." The man didn't pay any attention to her underline: if you have the effrontery to intrude. He trotted after them, wagging his gratefulness. "Thank you, thank you I'd like to, Miss Agnew."

Hank strode ahead, the bell sheep of a motley parade, the lead fool. Kitten had been a terrified child last night; he'd believed her bogies. She'd been afraid of the dark. There was no fear in her now. He'd been taken in although he knew better, knew that an actress must act. She'd acted better than she knew; he had been possessed; he had become Cavanaugh, the doughty knight, horsed with decision to rescue the suffering lady. Yet she was not to blame for his enchantment. He had wanted to play knight, wanted to sop his conscience with a mock rescue.

He damned her; he damned Les Augustin who had made her known to him. He would pipe them to Les's quarters and he would leave them there, Les and Kitten, to devour each other with vanity and malice. Gratia—Gratia had wandered out of her dream world; she must go back quickly before she lost her way. Let her return to her room and her book. Let the stranger disappear as unwanted as he had appeared. He, Hank, would go get drunk, forget all of them.

He wanted it to be answered that way, the easy way. Absolving him from participation. But when he entered the Pullman where was Les's compartment, Kitten moved in behind his shoulder. She asked, "What's your hurry?" She spoke lightly but her breath was caught back and her eyes avoided the closed door of drawing room A. She was not exorcised of fear. It was so near the surface, a touch and it would fester.

He had known he was wrong; it was corroborated. He said, "I'm in a hurry for a drink. What's wrong with that?"

She laughed as if he'd amused her, as if she were hiding the fact that he'd passed her safely beyond drawing room A. Her hand was under his arm as they reached Les's compartment. He couldn't leave her and go away. Even if she weren't touching him, he couldn't go away now.

The afternoon went slowly past the leaden windows. Drear world outside; inside Les's compartment noise and smoke and the filling of glasses. But there wasn't merriment, even the laughter was gray.

All through the long afternoon, he watched Kitten. Gratia and Les, together, watched Kitten. Even the outsider, Sidney Pringle, miserable here but clinging to human companionship, watched Kitten. Kitten preened and pranced and curled. She was the one thing alive under the weight of the afternoon. Alive but not real; she was a thing, glittering, empty. One word and she would be still. Hank knew the word. It was on his tongue and he was carefully silent fearing that it might roll off into sound. Les knew it; he juggled it high into silence each time he spoke. Sidney Pringle didn't know; he was outside. Gratia didn't know. She was protected by her dream.

In late afternoon the moving windows were slowly stilled. Les said, "La Junta." He said it wearily as if the train had been creeping all day. All of them looked out at the lorn station. No one walked on the platform with brisk, proud steps as at other stations. Snow like salt was shaken over the lowering dusk. Kitten shivered and turned from it to the warm lighted room just as Sidney Pringle said, "La Junta. Five o'clock."

She echoed, "Five o'clock."

The room wasn't warm. It was colder than the wintry air leashed outside. Because in that moment something licked out from behind her eyes. Something fearful to see.

She moved closer to Hank. She was quivering like a fine wire. It was Les who asked, "What happens at five o'clock Kitten?"

The something had scuttled into hiding almost before it had been visible. Kitten's voice was brittle, amused. "Tiresome. Viv asked me to drop in."

"You're going to?" Hank slid the question over his drink.

She answered him alone. "Don't worry. I'll take Mike with me."

"Maybe I'd better go along," Hank said slowly. "Jehovah wants to see me too."

Les added, "Why not? Let him—" His voice scraped. Whatever he'd been about to say had been wrong, so wrong that he was rigid.

Then Kitten said it for him. She'd known. *Kill two birds with one stone.* And her laugh was too shrill.

Only those words were spoken; unspoken was the great cloud that had hung over them all this afternoon. But the nebulous had taken shape. Kitten was afraid. And everyone in the little room was afraid with her. Even Gratia and Pringle, who didn't know the shape of fear was Vivien Spender, were fearful.

Kitten said, "No." Her head was high and in that moment she seemed to have a courage that made her truly beautiful, not just outwardly so. It might not be courage, it might be arrogance only, but her eyes were bright and there was color in her cheeks. She said no. She would walk alone. "It's business, Hank."

"So's mine."

"I want to get it over with," she said.

He understood the implication. This was between her and Viv Spender; she would face it. Facing it was better than enduring longer. He wasn't happy at her decision. He'd seen dying men sparked with the same sudden flare of courage. But he growled, "Go on then. Get it over with."

Kitten's laugh was reckless. "I'm going to finish this drink first. You can't rush me. He can wait."

Viv Spender could wait but she couldn't. She finished the drink in quick gulps. She pressed the great ruby into the hollow of her breasts as her satin hips shimmered across the room. At the door she smiled. "I won't be long." She went quickly and the dark, cold world outside pressed against the windows. All pretense of brightness went with her. Hank said heavily, "God."

No one asked where he was going as he too drained his glass and left the room.

FIVE

THIS WAS THE LONG afternoon, the impassable afternoon. This was the afternoon when tempers wore thin, when the buzzers sounded with increasing frequency, when restlessness stalked the Chief. The dry sere of late autumn was over the barren countryside; it was snowing up ahead in La Junta. The warmth and green of California was a resentment because it was too far away to be real.

By the time night fell, there would be renewal of the fiesta spirit of the Chief. There would be lights and clatter of voices and the clink of ice, the splash of soda. There would be rebirth of gaiety. The atavistic fear of the wasteland shut away by the dark. The city would be just around tomorrow's corner. The end of inaction. The Century waiting to transport them to the promised isle, to Manhattan.

Tomorrow James Cobbett would sleep in a bed, a warm woman, a good woman beside him; he would forget for a few brief days the rasp of summoning bells, the demands of strangers.

It was time for him to go to dinner. Tomorrow he could choose what he would eat out of his appetite, not from a menu. Tomorrow he would be at home.

—2—

Mike came to his room after lunch. She said, "Kitten wants me to sit in on your meeting. She wants everything in black and white."

She expected him to be angry. She was waiting for it. When he spoke genially, she relaxed. "I was going to ask you the same thing, Mike. I too want a witness."

He hugged secret satisfaction watching the change in her. Whatever suspicions she may have had of his purpose in seeing Kitten, he had dissipated. She couldn't have suspected the true purpose; he had given nothing away. Nor would he.

The wariness in her eyes these two days was out of anxiety for him, not knowing he had the resolution of Kitten's case in hand. He couldn't tell her; if she worried, that was the price she paid for not having faith in his ability to solve a problem. But it was well she would be present. He himself should have thought of that. He could have no better witness to his character than Mike.

She said, "Good," and she made no effort to hide her relief. "See you about five then."

The hour dropped out of his mouth like a bitter pellet. "Five?"

"Kitten said fivish."

His voice was carefully controlled. "I said after dinner."

"She can't come then." The wariness was again on her mouth. "If you're busy—"

He cut her off. "I won't be busy." He held his rage in checkrein. Until Mike had gone. Kitten had dared change the hour. Without consulting him she had set an impossible hour. He must chart his plans all over again. He could not offer her after-dinner coffee at five o'clock. She could not be expected to go to bed at that hour.

In his wrath he was half-way to the door before he recognized the danger of seeking her now. He had made a mistake going to her room this morning. It hadn't been a part of the plan, it had been out of anger. And it had been dangerous.

He had been seen going there. He hadn't noticed the slit of open door on his way. He'd been blanked out with the anger. It was on his return that through the slit he saw the prying eyes poked out of a pudgy little face. The eyes were malevolent with hate. He didn't know why they should be; the face was strange to him. But he knew he was recognized. It wasn't until he was again in his room that he remembered it was the face of the man who'd sat across from him in the diner, the fellow who made obnoxious noises in his soup. Why he should hate Vivien Spender, Vivien Spender couldn't imagine. It didn't disturb him.

He might have had a stray quaver of relief that he had not laid hands on Kitten. The man who hated would have been eager to tattle. It was true that in his anger, Viv had stalked to her room wanting to twist life out of her insolent body. Once there, his superior intellect had triumphed over animal rage. She wasn't worth the brief pleasure it would have given him. The moment he saw her and her dread, he was satisfied to wait. The final satisfaction would be as sweet accomplished by wit as by the laying on of hands.

He hoped she sensed that she was going to die. He wanted her to suffer, to try to inch her way out of the oncoming juggernaut of her deserved fate. He didn't believe she was acute enough to realize. Yet her fear of him had a physical stench, as if she were already touched with decay.

It must be accomplished this afternoon. He could wait no longer. The frustration was making him nervy. He would have to serve drinks instead of coffee. A strong drink should disguise an alien flavor as well as a hot bitter fluid. He would make certain she received the proper glass. It might be well to prepare a special cocktail, to cloud all the glasses with the mixture. Kitten couldn't resist a fancy drink. Drop a cherry in a glass and she'd suck the dregs. He'd order some maraschinos early from Charles. It would go off just as well in the afternoon as at night.

If Kitten returned to her room to sleep off some of her drinks, no one would be suspicious. He must make certain that Kitten did return to her room.

She must not be discovered until too late. There must be no chance of her being rushed to a hospital in the wilderness of Kansas. If Mike were free she could keep Gratia out of the way. Mike couldn't be in two places at once; nevertheless, Gratia must be kept away.

Everything fell into place concisely. He would see Gratia now; he would invite her to dine with him. If she met him in the club car at six, quarter to, she would be kept free of danger. After dinner, return here for talk, for planning her future. He could plan for her now; Kitten was already eradicated save for the act.

His finger rested on the buzzer but he put no pressure there. He would do this himself, no need to let Mike know. He wanted no middle man on this matter. Particularly he didn't want Mike and her unspoken warnings. Momentarily rage against Mike bit him. She had dared couple his name with that of the notorious Doumel.

This was the afternoon lull. The corridor outside was sound-less. He could knock on Gratia's door; it was business. It didn't matter if he was seen but he wouldn't be seen. He stepped out-side.

In the corner, Cobbett sat motionless on his leather seat. Viv was as startled as if guilt were written on his brow. Cobbett didn't look at him but he knew Viv was there, Viv strode past but he didn't stop at Gratia's door. He walked out of the car, con-scious that Cobbett's eyes followed him.

What business had the porter to sit there outside his room, a dark, silent jailer? What business had he to hold his eyes level with Viv's when he spoke to him? Did the damn coon think he was as good as Vivien Spender? He'd find out. Viv could have him fired tomorrow.

The knuckles of his fist were sharp on Mike's door. He didn't wait for her response; he strode into her compartment.

When she saw his face, her eyes blanked. She asked, "What is it?" Her voice, despite her effort to make it normal, was blank as her eyes.

It was an effort to wrench himself out of the tongs of his anger. He was a little shaken when he smiled. "I want to see Gratia Shawn."

Her breath came out in a gust. "I thought something was wrong."

He laughed at her. "Nothing's wrong. Except I don't care to have my business bruited about the train. I'll see her here."

She made the sheaf of papers neat: "I'll see if I can find her." He couldn't discover her face, her shoulder was turned to him. She went out, her face still hidden.

He turned his to her mirror. There was no trace of anger remaining on it. It was strong and handsome, and calm. He took up a magazine of Mike's. He read a few jumbled pages on radar before she returned, alone. He was carefully controlled now. He waited for her report; she withheld it, as if she were afraid to speak. He asked, smiling, "Well?"

"She isn't in her room," Mike said. She avoided his eyes.

"Where is she?"

She said, "I couldn't find her." She was lying.

He was ironic. "Maybe you didn't look very far."

She faced him now and her nostrils flared. She said, "She's in Les Augustin's room. They're all in there, Kitten and Hank Cavanaugh and Sidney Pringle. I asked the porter." Her mouth was rigid. "I didn't think you'd care to have Les Augustin knowing your business."

Mike didn't know what churned in him. He was so well

controlled. He said, "You're absolutely right." He walked to the door before he realized he was crushing her magazine in his fingers. He flung it away. "I'd like Gratia to meet me in the club car about six. For a drink and dinner after. Get word to her."

He didn't hear Mike's answer. He walked back to his own car. Cobbett was still sitting in his observatory, motionless, silent, aware. Viv strode past him without a glance. Without striking a blow.

—3—

He had said: I want a witness. It was said and her relief was great. Because he wasn't planning anything. He wouldn't have her present if there were a plan. It could be that wisdom had penetrated his anger. It could be only temporary reprieve. But the reprieve was relief so great that she returned to her compartment physically weak.

There was routine to occupy her this afternoon. Her work traveled with her. She didn't need to think, she didn't want to think. When the knock came at her door, her nerves knotted. It couldn't be that anything had happened. He entered before she could call out. Her surprise at seeing him was stifled by recognition of the condition he was in. The rage that jutted from his face couldn't be hidden; anyone who passed him. would be frightened by it. She was frightened but not for herself. For him and the danger to him if he had been observed.

He covered the poison quickly. He wanted her to bring Gratia Shawn to him. The cool request didn't match the heat of his emotion. She couldn't ask what had roused him; he believed he was under control when he spoke.

She went out, wondering, still frightened. Could he have already met with Kitten? She knew of no one else who drove him into such passion.

The corridor of his car was empty save for the porter resting on a small leather seat. She approached the door of drawing room B as if she were not afraid to enter it: Her knock was unanswered and she opened the door not daring to think what she might find. Her mouth trembled when she found nothing. No one. An empty room. She stepped back and closed the door. She stood there for a moment, holding to the latch, gathering the shattered pieces of her confidence into some semblance of a whole.

Standing there, she heard the jet of laughter, of Kitten's laughter, from behind another door. She was all right again, hearing Kitten. Kitten was untouched. Mike turned to go but she hesitated. The porter would know. She might as well ask; it would save combing the train. In his present humor, Viv was capable of sending her into the engine for information.

She went nearer to the porter. He was a solemn fellow, unlike the quick smiling Rufe of her car. "Do you by any chance know where Miss Shawn is?" she inquired.

He rose to answer her. "Both of the young ladies are in D, Mr. Augustin's compartment. Mr. Cavanaugh and Mr. Pringle are also there."

It was as if he knew the reason for her inquiry, knew as well that she must not seek Gratia in Augustin's room. He couldn't know but there was too much wisdom in his eyes.

She said, "Thanks. I won't bother them now," and she went back to Viv. He thought he received her report well; he didn't know the way he tortured the magazine in his hands.

When he had gone, she picked up the magazine where he had flung it, tried to smooth the pages. Her hands began to shake, her whole body was shaking as if she had been taken by malaria. This wasn't Viv. He wasn't himself; he was ill. He needed her help and she ached to help him. But she didn't dare, not unless he summoned her. She was only his secretary.

But if she hadn't known that Kitten would not see Viv without her, she would have gone to his car, taken up her watch beside the porter.

The endless afternoon, the weary scene pasted to her moving window, tightened her nerves. She tried to read but the print wandered from her eyes. She knew there was unpleasantness to be faced; she'd seen both Viv and Kitten in rage, separately and together. There was more than the unpleasant to face, there was the prevention of— She could not say the word. Not even to herself.

By five she was tight-lipped. She needed a drink to relax her; she was afraid to order. There wouldn't be enough time. The train was stopping at another lost station, shrunken under hard spits of snow. This was La Junta, there was yet the endless flatness of Kansas to cross but it would be mercifully shrouded in night.

By five-thirty the window pane was pricked by lights in the dreary darkened world outside. And Kitten did not come. Fear swelled in her. She had closed her mind to the slyness Viv might use to escape her resistance. She knew him, why had she believed he meant her to be present? He'd managed to see Kitten alone once today; he'd manage it again if that were his will and his plan.

She waited until near six. Her room was dark, it must have been cold, her hands and feet were numb. Only then did she realize; she hadn't delivered his message to Gratia. She had legitimate reason for returning to that car, for going to Augustin's room, looking for Kitten as well as Gratia. She had legitimate reason to go to Viv. If only she weren't too late. She caught up her purse and she ran, ran as if she raced with Death, and as if Death were the fleeter of foot.

—4—

One step took him into the corridor, the door clacked loudly after him. She was standing outside the door of drawing room A. She was alone. She didn't look frightened now; she had the insolent air of a high-priced prostitute. In the strange light and shadow of the corridor, the black satin of her dress writhed about her flesh. The cabochon ruby was a bloody stone hung upon her breast. The sharp sound of the door he had slammed stayed her hand. Her head turned and her frown discovered him.

She said with annoyance, "What do you want?"

He was belligerent. "Where's Mike?"

Behind her Cobbett sat on the small leather seat and ignored them. Cobbett was so entirely a fixture in the corridor that they could quarrel in his hearing without realizing he heard.

Her golden hair shimmered as she tossed her head. "I decided I'd see him alone."

He'd overcome the moment of cowardice which had held him to his drink as she left the compartment. The moment when he'd told himself she would be safe without a nosy stranger interfering. He wouldn't knuckle under to the cowardly way again. He said, "I'm going along."

"I don't want you." There were rude amber flecks in her brown eyes. She didn't want him because he reminded her of her fear. She'd tossed fear over her shoulder like a spill of salt and she didn't want it shaken on her again.

He said, "I don't care what you want. Spender sent for me and I'm on my way to see him. If you prefer to be private, get out of the way and I'll go alone."

He rattled his fist against the door as he spoke. She didn't get out of the way, she turned her eyes round and full on him. But she'd veered again on the wind of her fear. She hadn't the sureness her arrogance implied.

The door opened before she formed a new insult on her lips.

It didn't open wide. The man within wasn't visible to Hank, Kitten filled the aperture. He heard the rich voice, "Hello, Kitten. I've been waiting for you."

She stepped in, the door would have closed but Hank was too quick. He took her place in the opening and his eyes were level with the eyes of Vivien Spender.

The surprise in his was reflected in Spender's. Spender didn't understand what he was doing there. Hank didn't understand why he had accepted her brand of murderer for Spender. This man was not a murderer. He was a good-humored man, a big man. Not alone physically, his reactions were keen. You could see the intelligence that was stored in his skull, one look in the man's eyes gave the insight.

Hank hadn't met the man on eye level in the diner last night, he'd barely glanced at him. Had he, he would have known that Kitten was embroidering a tale to fit some sly fancy of her own.

Hank said, "I'm Cavanaugh. You wanted to see me."

Spender's eyes cleared. His voice was hearty. "Yes, I did, Mr. Cavanaugh. I hardly expected Kitten to bring you along with her—"

Kitten interrupted viciously, "I didn't bring him. He came." She curved herself down on the couch, one silken leg drawn under her. "You get rid of him."

Spender laughed in good humor. "Your bad manners are childish, Kitten. I'm delighted to have Mr. Cavanaugh. Come in and sit down."

He was a perfect host, as perfect as if he were in his Beverly home, not on the Chief. He was freshly shaved, his dark suit was newly pressed. There was a tray on a stand, glasses, a cocktail shaker, a small bowl of cherries in maraschino.

"I was just about to have a drink," he said. "You'll join me?"

"Certainly." Hank let himself down beside Kitten.

She was watching Spender. Her eyes were steady and smooth as polished stones.

"Kitten?" Spender took up the silver shaker, shook it.

For a breath her eyes held on the moving shaker. She said defiantly, "I'll have one if you do."

"I'll have two," Spender smiled. "This is a new recipe. Fortunately the steward in the club car had all the ingredients. Where's Mike?"

Hank's eyelids drooped. There was a change, an almost imperceptible change in Spender's voice before he asked the question. But the man's face was as open as before.

Kitten said, "I haven't any idea. Give me a cigarette, Hank?"

The hands on the shaker pressed a little more tightly, that was all. The voice was calm. "We'll have to wait for her before taking up our business. My secretary, Mr. Cavanaugh. Indispensable." He was as equal with Hank as if Hank too were clean-shaven, fresh-groomed. As if Hank too were an important and expensive executive. "I scarcely dare mix a cocktail without her permission."

He carried the glass to Kitten, dark, wine-colored liquid, a cherry supine in its somber depths: Kitten took it from him but didn't lift it to her lips. The stem wavered in her fingers. She wore the wrong lipstick, Hank hadn't seen it before; her face was too white for that color of wet blood. He shoved his spine upright. He had seen something else without seeing; Spender had masked the cocktail tray as he poured.

Hank said, "If you don't want it, give it to me." He took the glass out of her fingers. They uncramped slowly, one by one as if they had been frozen. He held the cocktail steady a brief second, waiting for Spender to knock it from his hand. Spender didn't stop filling the second glass. He handed it to Kitten.

Hank drank. If Spender were a murderer, too careful to give himself away even if a stranger must die, it didn't matter much.

The cocktail tasted like a concoction, too much bitters, slightly medicinal. He finished the drink and he didn't writhe in agony. Nothing wrong although what a man of the obvious good taste of Vivien Spender was doing messing up good liquor in this fashion, he didn't understand.

Kitten watched him drink, then put her own glass to her lips. Viv Spender, his glass in hand, took his place by the window. He tasted, made a slight grimace. "Why I waste good liquor this way! I'm incurably curious about recipes." He tasted again. He was urbane, pleasant. "I understand you're just back from the Orient, Mr. Cavanaugh. No doubt you met some rare recipes there."

Hank's eyes blackened. "No doubt." His words came from between his teeth. No doubt. Blood and filth and dead babies and two grains of rice. Hunger and grief and fear and two grains of rice. He didn't hear Spender's amiable recitation of what the man had found in the Orient before war. Rare recipes. He hadn't rooted through garbage for two grains of rice. If Hank had heard he would have risen and destroyed Spender. But his eardrums were split with remembered sound, the sound of the agonized, waiting for death. He said thickly, "Give me another drink."

"Certainly, Mr. Cavanaugh." Viv Spender was too big for the smallness of a train room. He was across to Hank before he had finished speaking. He took the glass and refilled it at the table tray, returned it to Hank. "Kitten?"

She withdrew imperceptibly from the tower of him. She looked into her drink. Her fingers dipped into the dregs and lifted out the wet cherry. She was studiedly rude as she pushed the glass at him. "Yes, give me another." She put the cherry in her mouth and sucked it.

Hank gulped. Drink it quick; it didn't taste so foul if you drank it quick. It was bringing the fog. It was dulling the spikes of memory. Fleetingly he remembered his fears before he tasted the first. He gave a loud laugh, loud and harsh. From the table Spender looked quickly at him out of puzzled eyes. Kitten drew her silken legs away, distaste narrowing her nose.

He laughed to recall how he'd thought Spender was offering him poison. Spender was giving him the best cure, the only cure, with his filthy concoction. It was strong drink and that was what he needed. That was what the doctor ordered. Take it strong and you didn't need so many, you could blur out quicker. Tasty little cocktail. A rare recipe. Must ask Spender what was in it. One third whisky, one third brandy, one third raw alcohol?

"Some drink," Hank laughed. "A rare old drink." He was drunk and it was good. He couldn't remember why he wanted to be drunk and that was good.

Spender said, "Let me give you another." The big man, the big important man was coming over to give drunken bum Cavanaugh another glass of his rare recipe. He was carrying Kitten's brimming glass; it looked pretty with the cherry plopped in it.

Hank pronounced a solemn edict. "Cherries take up room."

Kitten screamed.

He flailed his way out of the fog. Viv Spender was going to kill Kitten. Before his eyes, before his cowardly closed eyes. But she wasn't dead. She was livid with rage. Her mouth was the mouth of a guttersnipe. "You clumsy oaf!"

Spender said, "I'm sorry."

The Chief had swayed. The Chief had rounded a curve, had clattered unevenly over a hump in the roadbed. Kitten's drink was upside down in her black satin lap. The cherry was brightly embossed on the wide grotesque of the stain.

"I'm awfully sorry," Spender said.

Kitten kicked him out of the way. She put the cherry in her mouth and she stood up, letting the cocktail glass splinter to the floor. What she said was out of the gutter. Rage carried her from the room; rage made her walk unsteadily or she too had had too many drinks.

Spender was on his knee gathering the broken glass. He said, "Damn clumsy of me."

Hank smiled blissfully. He didn't have to worry about Kitten now. She wouldn't come back here in a hurry. He could close his eyes and fog out.

—5—

Mike pushed open the door without knocking. Viv was by the window, drink in hand, conversation in his mouth. On the couch was Hank Cavanaugh, his eyes closed, his mouth smiling. He was drunk.

Mike said, "Where's Kitten?" It didn't sound like her voice. It grated from her throat.

Viv said, "She went to change her dress." He grinned, a little sheepish his grin. "I spilled a cocktail on her."

Mike's knees wobbled. She put her hand on the chair back. "She didn't come for me. I was afraid—" She sucked the words in, made others to replace them. "I was afraid she'd forgotten the appointment with you."

"Not at all," Viv smiled. "She and Cavanaugh arrived together a bit after five. After the mishap, she rushed away quite upset. Meantime Cavanaugh and I have had quite a talk."

Hank Cavanaugh opened his eyes. "You talked. I didn't listen." He didn't look drunk now that his eyes were open. They weren't glazed. They were sardonic. He turned them on Viv. "It's taking Kitten a long time to change her dress."

Viv sighed. "I've known Kitten to spend an hour putting on her hat. God knows when she'll be back."

Hank pulled up his knees, set his heels on the floor. "She's not coming back," he said.

Mike's hands went cold. Viv was looking at Hank, looking at him in silence. Again her voice wasn't her own. "Why not?"

"She was too mad. He spoiled her best dress."

Viv's mouth opened and he laughed long. "She'll be back. With a bill. For a dress three times as expensive." He looked regretful. "It won't help my expense account."

Hank was on his feet. "If she comes back, tell her I'm in Augustin's. If she comes there, I'll tell her you want to buy her an olive branch with a new dress on it. An expensive one."

"Not too expensive," Viv said good-naturedly. "You won't have another drink?"

Hank's smile was ironic. "No more of those. They're poison."

Again her eyes leaped to Viv's silence, to the painted quality of his good nature. His voice was easy. "We'll talk over that contract in New York?"

"Sure," Hank said and the irony was bitter. "With a rare recipe."

He went out leaving silence. She didn't know how to break it. Now that he was gone, Viv had stopped pretending. His knuckles were hard. A train shuddered past the dark windows hurtling westward. The dissonance shook her but it broke the spell of silence. Viv said calmly, "Offensive bastard. Is he worth going after?"

She nodded. "Tops in his field."

"Drunkard. Don't know if I want him."

Nothing had happened. Viv was unchanged. Kitten had taken Hank Cavanaugh for protection; she hadn't needed Mike. Mike's relief edged her voice. "I'd like a drink myself, Viv."

"Sure." He opened a traveling case. "You don't want that stuff." He nodded to the cocktail shaker. "I mixed it for Kitten." He took out a fresh pinch bottle, began removing the foil.

She watched his moving hands while doubt again thorned her. She had to know. Her tongue was dry. "I'd like to sample it."

Could he hear the ragged beat of her heart? "Your specials are usually pretty good stuff."

There was no hesitation. "Sample it at your own risk. If Cavanaugh left any to be sampled." He coiled away the foil neatly. "That's another reason I'm not sure I want him under contract. A man who could keep on drinking that sort of concoction can't have any taste."

She didn't need to drink now. There was no more doubt. All was well, somehow Viv had been saved from his nightmare. She poured a bit into a glass, swallowed it. Her mouth twisted wryly.

Viv was amused. "Now will you deny it's poison?"

—6—

When he opened the door the scene was frozen exactly where he had left it. Gratia by the window, her quiet face reflected in the shining black of the pane; her head resting against the seat back. Her eyes were wide on him as they had been when he left the room, as they had been all afternoon. Sometime during the afternoon they'd lost regret. As if she'd come to a realization of what motivated his acts, as if understanding were again between them.

Les was beside her, motionless as before. Pallid, weary, clinging to her peace. Drawing it into himself because his need was great.

Set apart, solitary, was Sidney Pringle, his head bent, his eyes on the floor. Waiting to be told when he could speak.

Les opened his eyes when Hank entered. Hank saw then, Les hadn't been as listless this afternoon as he feigned. His eyes were sharp. His voice was as sharp. "Where's Kitten?"

Mike had asked the same question with the same hidden fright.

Hank closed the door. He'd been drunk; he wasn't now. He

felt good, just right. He said, "Changing her dress. Spender dumped a cocktail on her."

Les eyed him, accepted truth. "Oh, no." Mirth began to quiver his nose. "Oh, no!"

"It was an accident," Hank said. Their eyes met again and they laughed together. They needed a laugh. The long watch was over. It had ended in a joke. Les asked, "Did you get a job?" Hank laughed some more. "Do you think I want his jobs?"

Sidney Pringle raised his eyes to Hank. They were matted with hatred. His voice quavered. "Your suit needs pressing. Worse than mine does. You don't have to worry about how you look because you're important. You didn't care whether you saw Vivien Spender or not. You can turn down his money. You don't have to sell neckties."

Hank raised an oblique eyebrow. Les closed his eyes. Outside the window a train shuddered by.

Sidney Pringle said, "I'm Sidney Pringle. I wrote *Asses' Milk*. It's about a little man who tried to get out of the tenements, about me! I wrote it at nights on a kitchen table. After selling neckties all day in a bargain basement. It took me out of the basement. It took me to Hollywood."

He couldn't stop talking. It didn't matter whether they wanted to hear or not, he would tell it. He'd touched bottom of despair. Because Hank Cavanaugh had turned Vivien Spender down.

"It wasn't my fault I couldn't write there. The industry is too big, too capitalistic to recognize art." Hysteria reddened his voice. "They think writing is something to be turned out like cheap neckties, so many words an hour, so many pages a day. They wouldn't let me create. It wasn't my fault I failed."

His chin was shaking like jelly. "Art isn't creation to Vivien Spender, to any of those great tomcat producers. Art is a body in a bed. It isn't a man's life blood drying in a pen while he sells neckties in a bargain basement." His knuckles rubbed tears into his eyes.

"She didn't have to tell Vivien Spender about me. I didn't ask her to. She brought it up herself. And she lied to me. She said she couldn't ask favors. Not for me. She didn't look over her shoulder at me the way she did at you. She didn't call me 'Darling' and make the word a promise that quivers in a man's stomach. She didn't even speak to me at the table last night. I wasn't good enough for her. I wasn't important." His voice trembled to frenzy. "I was a failure. If I'd been important she would have twisted her body at me. She would have called me darling. She would have taken me with her to see Viv Spender. She—"

Les interrupted. His voice was soft but the line of his mouth was vicious. "Shut up."

Hank threatened, "Don't talk about her as if she weren't coming back."

Sidney Pringle didn't know; he had no idea of what the rest of them had been through this day. He didn't know about anything but himself. He began to cry. Gratia turned her eyes away from the obscenity.

Hank said, his voice rising, "If you'd go where I've been and see what I've seen, you'd stop feeling sorry for yourself." He didn't care how blameless Pringle was; the man had roiled the waters again.

Pringle wept, "I'm not sorry for myself. I just don't want to sell neckties."

Les chanted tonelessly, "You don't want to sell neckties. Kitten doesn't want to sing in cheap bars. I don't want to cadge meals and sleep in subways. We'd rather die first." He began to laugh and then he began to cough, he couldn't stop coughing. When he took his handkerchief away from his mouth, there was a spat of blood on it. He covered it with furtive quickness. Hank alone saw.

He was violent. "She's all right. I know she's all right. I was there all the time. She's just changing her dress. It takes her a long time to change her dress." He swung around to the opening door.

Mike was motionless on the threshold. He was afraid for her to speak; everyone was afraid to hear her speak. Except Pringle. Pringle sniffled.

She began, "Gratia, Viv wants you to have dinner with him."

Les said, "No." His arm moved out to block Gratia's way. He wasn't languid now; he was tightly knotted as a wire. This was what he'd been expecting. It was for this he'd husbanded his strength, to keep Gratia safe, to keep her away from Vivien Spender.

Hank repeated, "No." He stuck out his jaw as if it were Spender who stood there, not a paid emissary. "You're too late, Gratia's having dinner with us." He was filled with a savage triumph. Without putting it to words he understood now the motivation of Les's personal, unmotivated feud with Spender. The man had too much too easily, his accretion of power was a denial of the inherent rights of all other men. To best him even in this small way was a renewing of manhood.

Mike didn't protest the decision. She was passive as a stranger. She said, "I'll tell him." And she went away.

Gratia was unsure. "Perhaps I should—"

"Darling!" Les's fingers closed over her wrist. "You promised us."

"Let's have a drink," Hank offered. He knew there'd been too much drinking; with it came the ugly hypertension. But he didn't know what else to say.

"I don't want a drink." Gratia was pleasant but definite. "I'm hungry."

"Stick with us until Kitten comes back and we'll eat right away," Hank suggested. It was hard to speak the words, so hard the palms of his hands were wet. He wiped them on his trousers.

Sidney Pringle piped with wounded dignity, "I ought to go. You want me to go."

"Why does everyone want to go?" Hank roared it out. "What you need is another drink, Sid. Then you can tell me all over again about how you come to write *Asses' Milk*. Damn good book, you know."

Pringle tried to smile. "If I take another drink I'll be drunk."

"You're drunk already." Hank was playing a part because he couldn't bear the waiting; he was hanging on to the miserable Pringle because he alone was solid in this nebula of fear; he alone, outside of it, was normal.

Gratia spoke again with that same pleasant definiteness. "I'll go tell Kitten to hurry."

"No!"

They said the word together, Les and Hank, said it so quickly. They were afraid for their eyes to meet.

Gratia said firmly, "I want to wash up before dinner." She glanced at the bracelet of Les's hand on her wrist. Slowly he unloosed it.

She stood up. They couldn't stop her; they couldn't go with her. She was capable of walking a few steps to her drawing room, of washing her own hands and face. She couldn't help but sense their unspoken reluctance for her to go; it swirled in thick clouds about them stifling their words.

Les could speak if he hadn't forgotten how. He could drop those polished pebbles from his smiling mouth, he could delay her a little longer. Hank couldn't speak. Not without giving birth to the monstrous obsession which lay like a stone in his stomach and his brain.

It was Les who answered her, answered gravely, "Yes. We very much want her to hurry."

She accepted his words. She smiled her lovely smile. They watched her cross the little room. She opened the door and took a deep breath, a clean breath. "I won't be a minute," she smiled.

He couldn't let her walk in on it. He called, "Wait!"

She remained where she was, puzzled, obeying only because his word was a command. He wasn't that kind of a coward. He had to be the one to go.

He felt Les behind him in the doorway. Hank's hands were rough as he pushed Gratia aside, pushed her to Les Augustin. He said nothing, there was nothing now to say. There was nothing to do but face the specter of a lost fight. He walked forward steadily. He didn't compromise with his prescience. Without knocking, he opened the door and went in.

SIX

JAMES COBBETT WATCHED WITH them all afternoon. Not because he was interested in them; because he was heavy, because
he'd been unable to shake off the weight of depression which had
settled on him when the Chief left L.A. yesterday noon.

His passengers had been quiet enough during the long afternoon. Surfeited with the squirrel-tread movement of the train,
they'd closed themselves behind their doors. Too lethargic even
for bell ringing. He understood the hopelessness of travelers
this second day out. Familiarity with ceaseless motion reduced
the high speed of the Chief to a tortoise crawl. The unchanging
horizon line of Arizona and New Mexico had the unending and
fearful sameness of crossing eternity. Engendering something
that bordered on atavistic fear. Moving, always moving; yet the
movement was to no avail. The scene pasted on the windows was
ever the same, wasteland and sky.

The bridal couple clung together behind their door. The journey to them was fleet as a falling star and as beautiful. If they had
recognized the resemblance to eternity, they would not fear. They
needed eternity to hold their happiness. The old couple drowsed
together, content with each other out of long habit. They had

weathered endless finite eternities; so many they no longer recognized one until it was past.

The others huddled together in their incongruity. All but Vivien Spender. He sat alone behind his door. James Cobbett learned one thing about Vivien Spender as he sat alone outside Spender's door. One thing that money and power and importance did for a man. It made him lone.

He learned another thing about Spender after a little. Even the great were not immune from the arid depression of the long afternoon. Spender came out of his room, left the car seeking human relations. Cobbett, not caring, learned who it was Spender sought. With the fact, he added to his knowledge of the lone, restless man. He could not go simply to Gratia Shawn as a poor man would go. He had to send his secretary.

When Spender returned to the car, a dark motif was added to the pattern of knowledge. The great could be unreasonable in the throes of anger. The look Spender darted at him was bleak with hatred.

After that the car was quiet. At four James Cobbett went to eat. Dinner didn't alleviate the heavy hanging over his head. He left the companionship of his own as quickly as he could, returned to his tired vigil. It might be that Rufe's good-natured taunt was a glimmer of truth. He had the ha'nts.

There was activity after five. Kitten Agnew at Spender's door. The man with the mouth worn in sardonic grooves, Cavanaugh, following her. Quarrelsome words; silence. The bride and bridegroom, clean and happy, hand in hand, moving forward doubtless to the club car for a before-dinner cocktail.

When Kitten came out of Spender's, Cobbett dropped his eyes quickly. Her mouth was an ugly blur, her pupils glazed. She came alone and she walked unsteadily to her own door, pushed inside. Something cold touched the root of his spine. He had looked upon something unclean. If he had been Rufe, he would have performed a superstitious ritual. James Cobbett was educated; he had no talisman to exorcise evil. He sat there in the silence and wondered.

He wondered about Vivien Spender and those who were lighted by the sun of Spender. He saw the secretary enter the car, hurrying as if fear nipped her heels. He saw Cavanaugh as he wavered out of Spender's room; scorn twisting his mouth. The crisscross of movement went on. Mike Dana came out shortly after Cavanaugh. She wasn't hurrying now, she moved like a wooden figure; she too went to Augustin's. In, out, in again. She returned to Vivien Spender. Cobbett saw her angular face, wooden as her body. He saw her hesitation at Spender's door, the fear line of white framing her lipstick. And he added to Vivien Spender, a man who could engender evil and scorn and fear. It wasn't good for a man to have too much.

In and out. The old financier and his blue-white diamond wife on their way to the diner. But Kitten didn't come out. James Cobbett was waiting for that, waiting to look on her again, to reassure himself of her humanness because he had no superstition for reassurance. No one went to her room; she remained closeted there alone.

He was still waiting when the other girl appeared, Gratia Shawn. The tightness of his muscles relaxed. He'd been a fool to sit here brooding all afternoon. Because he didn't feel quite himself, a cold coming on, a stomach upset. Because his lonesomeness for Mary and the children was never stronger than when he was nearing them.

Gratia Shawn ended his doldrums. She was young; she was cleareyed, smiling, human. The long afternoon was over, had been over since La Junta. He should have realized before. It was night and the Chief was coming alive. Tomorrow was the reality of Chicago. Everything was all right now.

And in the moment of realization came the denial. Gratia was halted, pushed aside by Cavanaugh. It was he who went to Kitten's door, who entered her room. In Augustin's doorway there was tableau, the girl and Augustin holding each other, behind them a triangle of Sidney Pringle's curious brow.

Cobbett didn't know why alarm rang in his head. Only that he'd been feeling lowdown and that he'd been the last one to look on the face of Kitten. He was the one who knew it wasn't her face but that of one possessed.

He remained on the leather seat but he was tensed waiting. He saw Cavanaugh return to the others, his face masked, expressionless. Cobbett watched. He didn't hear their words; they spoke quietly and they were at the opposite end of the corridor.

He watched them move like puppets, impelled by a will stronger than theirs. Cavanaugh and Augustin. The girl, forbidden, following after a moment. Pringle creeping up behind her. The four were a motionless frieze at the doorway of drawing room B.

James Cobbett didn't want to see what they looked upon. It was not his will that he rose quietly from his place and moved forward. Not his curiosity nor his anxiety. He was responsible for this car and its tenants. Something was wrong.

When he reached the group he didn't have to speak. They parted, made a lane through which he could walk to the threshold. He followed the flickering horror of their eyes to the floor of the drawing room.

A golden scarf flung there. The scarf of her hair. A pale mound crumpled in the darkness. One hand clenched.

Alarm was husky in his throat. "Is she—"

Cavanaugh spoke behind him. His voice grated flatly. "She's dead."

James Cobbett heard the words and knew them to be truth.

Kitten Agnew was dead. She was dead when she passed him in the corridor. Death was the evil which had possessed her.

—2—

Mike wanted to go. He wanted her to go. He didn't know why he kept her there, upright in the chair, inhuman as a sawdust doll, making pretense of attention to the empty words he spoke. He didn't know why he made an effort to entertain her, as if she were a chance acquaintance he wished to impress.

He knew only that he couldn't let her go like this, eaten with suspicion, without reason for suspicion. He deserved her trust; for years he'd had her absolute loyalty, he had no intention of accepting her repudiation now. She'd been all right after Cavanaugh left the room, after she'd made certain with her own mouth that Kitten's drink was harmless. She'd believed that Kitten had gone to change her dress.

He'd been clever, very clever. He'd poured the first drink for Kitten, a harmless if loathsome cocktail. She'd take a second; he knew that. He knew how to play on her, just how to put another drink in her hand.

She thought she was being clever; Kitten was transparent as cheap silk. Bringing Cavanaugh instead of Mike. A stranger, someone not under the influence of Vivien Spender. Poor, stupid Kitten. Having no faint recognition of how Viv could twine about his finger any person he set out to capture. Cavanaugh was on Viv's side almost at once. Idiot Kitten. As if a drunken newspaperman could hold out against a man of Spender's civilized nuances.

Cavanaugh took that first drink from her. Perhaps in her silly soul she'd had a premonition of danger. Viv prepared her second cocktail exactly as he'd planned her second. He'd rehearsed earlier, a careful rehearsal. He had no fear of being discovered now. He'd prepared for Mike; the most minute detail had been worked out to pass her scrutiny. He knew where to stand, where to place his hands, just when to empty the vial into the glass. It wasn't discernible in the concoction. A cherry for a fillip.

He watched her drink, watched with no emotion save appreciation of the interesting conversation he was developing for Cavanaugh's pleasure. Not that he needed to converse. One cocktail added to what Cavanaugh had already taken this day took care of the man.

He had planned the mishap. A cocktail upset on her dress and she'd go quickly to change. She'd be safe in her own room when the draught took effect. He knew just how long it would take, minimum and maximum. He'd learned that a long time ago. If by mischance any of her drinking companions went to her room, he'd think Kitten had, to be crude, passed out. There was little risk that any one of them would go to her. They'd been shut up all day in Les Augustin's room; they'd all be in about the same shape as Cavanaugh.

With the exception of Gratia. There was still the need to make certain of Gratia. When Mike admitted she hadn't carried out his orders to Gratia, his mouth tightened. His angry, "I don't care where she is, I want her now," was careless. Mike was too keyed to suspicion. She went at once to fetch the girl but she was reluctant to go.

He didn't know what happened in that room; he knew only that Mike returned with fear again sucking her blood. She said, "It's too late. Gratia has promised them."

He could have slashed her with blame but he held his tongue. He must not give way to anger again. If Gratia were remaining with Augustin and his friends, she wouldn't be retiring early.

He shrugged and asked playfully, "You won't desert too, Mike? Or have you more important fish to fry?"

She said, "I won't desert you, Viv." But she didn't match his mood. There was a great sadness on her homely mouth. A sadness that was not relieved by the entertainment he furnished for that purpose. The knock at the door was welcome relief. She shouldn't have been frightened by it; he wasn't. She shouldn't have moved board-stiff to answer.

She opened the door a handsbreadth. He waited calmly. He heard her say, "One moment." She closed the door before she turned to him. Behind the slant green glasses the emptiness of her eyes was shocking. She said, "It's Hank Cavanaugh. He wants to see you."

He breathed satisfaction. "Good. I knew he'd come around." His smile was sure. "A contract with Vivien Spender isn't something to refuse."

Into her empty eyes came the oil of pity.

He broke off. "What does he want?"

"He wants to see you." Her gesture was limp as chiffon. "Out there."

Something had gone wrong. Someone had stumbled across Kitten. Too soon. Too wisely.

He put a little laugh into his words. "I wonder what he wants that's so private." He stood up, his shoulders square, and crossed to the door; opened it smiling. When he saw Cavanaugh's face, he knew he was right.

Cavanaugh said, "I want to show you something."

He never felt more sure of himself than at that moment. Just the correct tilt to the eyebrows, the slight puzzlement to the lips. He didn't need words; pantomime was more expressive. He followed Cavanaugh.

They were waiting outside Kitten's door, the chance companions of her last journey. The brittle sophisticate, Les Augustin. The resentful failure, Sidney Pringle. The beautiful innocent, Gratia Shawn. All of them reduced by death to the common denominator of fear.

He went past them silently, following Cavanaugh to the doorsill. Only then did the swift horror come to his face. He cried, "Kitten." He snapped on the lights. "She's sick. Hurry. Get a doctor."

The cue was picked up with a startling suddenness. "I've sent for a doctor." It almost spoiled his performance. He shot a quick glance over his shoulder. It was James Cobbett who had spoken. He'd taken his place with the others. Mike too, her eyes a smudge of horror. They were all watching him with awful silence.

He stepped into the room at once, bent over her. "Someone help me." He picked her up; she was a slight burden as he lifted her to the couch, laid her there. "Look in the medicine cabinet. She's sick. Do something!"

They had closed him in. The doorway was a montage of their silent faces. Hank Cavanaugh's lips snarled softly, mockingly, "She isn't sick. She's dead."

Viv looked at all of them, one by one, as if the words had been incomprehensible. He turned away and looked down at what lay on the couch, what once had been Kitten Agnew. Slowly he lifted her wrist, felt for the pulse. His thumb pressed where there should be the life beat but where there was none. He dropped the slight wrist. "She's dead."

His mouth moved silently, his eyes stung. He tried to say something, words would not come. He dropped on his knees beside the couch and began to weep. It had been a fine performance. He buried his wet face on Kitten's satin breast. Above him he heard the thin wail that broke from Mike's throat.

—3—

Mike stood outside the door. Her face felt swollen as if she'd been weeping. She hadn't wept; she didn't know why she should want to weep for Kitten, why dry-eyed she should ache for tears.

She didn't know how she could face them. He should have come himself. He could have told them and made them believe. He was calm again, after those first moments of frenzied grief when she'd led him back to his room. Scant moments. She hadn't offered her breast as a wailing wall this time. But she'd remained with him, alone with him, alone with a murderer. She could have prevented him being a murderer. If she'd had the courage to tell him what she knew before the fact. Her silence had murdered Kitten. She sat there woodenly until his grief was spent.

By the time the officials came he'd assumed the proper proportions of regret and bewilderment, a touch of horror, a soupçon of grief. Untouched by his act, conscienceless, directing the scene. The doctor was a well known Los Angeles physician on his way to Chicago. Viv had had his way with him, with the conductors, with James Cobbett, Pullman attendant. There was no suspicion in any of them. They accepted him with readiness flavored with hidden awe, well hidden the awe. This was democracy, the great Spender asking a logical favor of railroad employees. He'd carried it off with his usual flair. Kitten would continue the journey as far as Chicago there in her drawing room. No one would know; the door locked. Everything was simple, everything efficient. If there were unplumbed depths in the dark eyes of James Cobbett, no one cared.

After they left, Viv sent her to Augustin's compartment. She knew she could not face them, she knew he was the one who should go. She could not refuse; habit was too strong.

The four faces that lifted to her entrance were four masks. Not even the eyes moved.

She said, "It was her heart."

Hostility fixed her against the door. Hostility from all. From Gratia huddled in a window corner; from Les Augustin, a coiled adder, beside her. From the poor misfit Kitten had lunched with, Sidney Pringle. From Hank Cavanaugh, tall, vengeful.

She forced herself to go on with the report. "The doctor said—"

Hank Cavanaugh's cruel mouth interrupted. "Viv Spender killed her."

The cry didn't come from her; it came from Gratia. Horror distended the girl's eyes. Sidney Pringle looked at Cavanaugh with beady curiosity.

Hank said loud, "She knew Viv Spender was going to kill her."

Gratia whispered, "I don't believe it. It isn't true." Agony twisted her face.

Mike cried, "He didn't. He couldn't have done it." She went over it carefully, so carefully again. Oh God, again. "You were there with her. There was nothing wrong with the cocktails. You drank them. He did. I did." Why didn't he help her, not stand there with that terrible smile? Didn't he know she was half crazy knowing it had happened, yet knowing it couldn't have happened? He was present. He wouldn't let it happen.

He said, "I don't know how it was accomplished. Only that it was."

"It was her heart." She was forced to defend Viv. Knowing it was murder but that he couldn't have murdered. "Go ask the doctor. It was her heart."

Hank said, "It stopped beating."

In the silence, no one breathed. The silence was too terrible even for them to endure. Les murmured, "I wonder if she'd taken an overdose of sleeping tablets. That stops a heart from beating."

She couldn't look at him. She'd given him the weapon herself, the knowledge of the pattern. It hadn't been repeated! Les couldn't use the knowledge.

Some strength seeped into her veins. She could complete her errand. "Viv wants you, Gratia."

Les's laughter was shocking. "Let him come here."

Hank echoed, "Let him come here."

It was a dare, let him come if he dare, come before this jury to be judged. He should have come in the first place. Only he could answer them. If he dared.

She said, "I'll tell him."

He'd done this to be safe. He wasn't safe.

—4—

She went back to him. He didn't know the sickness that possessed her. He looked up from his memoranda, Jovian peace on his broad brow, his eyes unblemished by thought or deed. When he saw she was alone a shadow, the faintest shadow crossed his face.

"Gratia?"

She wet her lips. "They want you to come there."

Anger flooded him. His control was on the surface, beneath it were the hairtrigger nerves. "They?"

She nodded. Words came hard. She named them. "Les Augustin. Hank Cavanaugh. Sidney Pringle."

"Who is Pringle?"

"He's a writer. I remembered the name this afternoon. We didn't pick up his option." She watched his mind. He wasn't worried about Pringle or the failure to take up an option. He could manage Pringle. Another option. He wasn't worried about Hank Cavanaugh. He'd already made advances there. He'd sign up those two. Les Augustin had been a wasp too long. He hated Augustin, and he knew he couldn't buy Augustin. Only for a million dollars. He might have to spend the million.

She wanted desperately to warn him, watching the cool calculation. He must not be crass before them, not at this time. He didn't know they were waiting for him with cold eyes, with open swords. He must realize when he saw them; he would play it right. He was never wrong.

He demanded, "What do they want?"

She said heavily, "I think you'd better go see them." He looked long at her. He wouldn't believe they knew the truth of him, not until he smelled their hostility. He must face it himself.

He said, as if humoring her whim, "Very well." He pushed aside his notes and slid out from the confining table. She was afraid to look at him when he stopped in front of her. He said, "You're right, Mike. I should talk to them." He put his hand on her shoulder. She held herself rigid, not daring to shrink from him. "You're so tired." His voice was kind; she alone knew that the kindness was only an empty cadence. "Why don't you go rest for a while?"

She lifted her eyes to his face. He wasn't trying to read her; he didn't know yet the prescription bottle that weighted her mind. She said, "I'll wait here for you."

—5—

Les Augustin, orchestra leader. Hank Cavanaugh, exile newspaperman. Sidney Pringle, writer. And Gratia, whose beauty caught your heart, even in this poignant withdrawal. How absurd to have been apprehensive of this meeting. Simply because Mike was so shattered by the past few hours that she hadn't the courage to face anyone, not even him.

It would be child's play to answer their questions. They weren't lying in wait for him. Their antagonism was open. It was only natural, after all, that they would be suspicious when Kitten was drinking with them one moment and was dead the next. It wasn't suspicion of him but of sudden events. If they got ugly, he'd fling a few suspicions himself. Her lunch with Pringle, her afternoon in this room. He too could wonder what had happened to Kitten.

He stood there at the doorway after he entered, tall, grave, in command of the situation. No one asked him to be seated; he would refuse if asked. He preferred to be the tower above them. He said, "Mike says you wanted to see me."

They said nothing. Their eyes were motionless on him.

He let his voice break a little. "Kitten is dead. Nothing I can do, nothing you can do, can bring her back to us." He paused for a reverent hush.

"The conductor has been kind enough to allow us to continue through to Chicago. I asked that boon. I didn't want her to be taken off at some lonely way station." He was doing well, a catch of breath now. "She wouldn't have liked that, being left alone in the dark, in a strange place."

Les's eyes were like a cat's. He murmured, *"Give her strewings . . ."*

Viv didn't understand. He continued, "The conductor has made one request. That no one on board learn of Kitten's death until after we reach Chicago." He queried gently, "You will respect his wish?"

"We wouldn't think of telling anyone." It was Hank Cavanaugh who spoke. Events had sobered him. "Would we, Les?" He was an ugly customer, his sarcasm was heavy handed.

Augustin's was light. "Certainly not." He blinked up at Viv Spender. "What happened to her, Viv?"

Viv controlled his knotting muscles. They knew what happened; Mike had told them. He'd sent her to tell them. "The doctors warned her months ago that she must take it easy. She was burning herself out, young as she was. Too much work—and play. She was too proud to believe them. Too headstrong to listen."

"You didn't expect her to die, did you, Viv?" Augustin asked. It wasn't a simple question; it was studiedly insolent.

He couldn't allow his anger to break through. "No. When she told me, I believed she was dramatizing." He moved cautiously although without seeming caution. "Kitten was always dramatic." His smile was saddened at the corners. "You know that. Yes I begged her to be careful. I asked her not to make this trip. I wanted her to take a vacation."

"A long vacation," Augustin slurred.

Kitten had talked too much. Viv said, "For her sake only." He went on, "If I'd had any idea that she—"

Hank Cavanaugh interrupted, "There'll be an autopsy in Chicago."

His eyebrows knotted. "An autopsy? Why should there be?"

Augustin smiled at Cavanaugh. "We didn't expect her to die. Not of heart failure."

He couldn't let them know he wanted to kill them. With violent hands. There was no reason for an autopsy. Kitten had died of heart failure. The doctor had certified it. She'd died too quickly for the sedative alone to be responsible. Her heart hadn't been strong enough to beat the minimum time. This macabre vaudeville team couldn't force an autopsy. Not that it would make any difference, only a change of sudden death to suicidal sudden death. Heart failure induced by an overdose of sedative.

He shook his head sadly. "I don't believe the doctor will force that ignominy on her. It would serve no purpose." Sadness became him. "This loss—I can't tell you what it means to me. I still don't believe it. That Kitten—" He swallowed the lump in his throat. A good rehearsal before meeting the Chicago press tomorrow. "The curtain has fallen."

Augustin's voice deliberately cut into the expected silence. *"The last act crowns the play."*

He nodded slowly. Not a bad line; he could use it tomorrow. But he didn't like the way the fellow was laughing, laughing without sound. He spoke quietly. "You won't mind sharing Mike's compartment tonight, Gratia? Your things have been moved."

Hank's harsh voice contradicted, "Gratia stays with us."

He waited for control. "I don't believe that's wise. There might be questions—"

Les Augustin repeated it, "Gratia stays with us."

He swallowed pride. He coaxed, "I don't believe it is wise for Gratia's career to stay with three men she scarcely knows. Innocent as it would be. Besides, she needs rest. Just look at her."

All of them looked at her. She was alone in her bewilderment, in her lack of understanding. The ordeal of death had hollowed her eyes, faded her color to parchment. She was never more beautiful. Viv yearned to comfort her.

Hank said slowly, "Don't worry about Gratia. We intend to take good care of her."

Augustin's gentleness turned from her and in turning became malice. "We intend to take very good care of her. No heart attack. No overdose of sleeping tablets."

It was said. It was for this they ordered him to come, to accuse. They could not know; they could not possibly know the form of the act. Even the doctor didn't know. There would never be proof. It was wise he had personally attended the moving of Gratia's things. And in attending had placed the emptied bottle of sleeping tablets in the bath cabinet. The pellets had been flushed away on the dark tracks. The first fright passed and in its wake he was left more secure than before. He could ignore their gauntlet. He was safe. He could use the suggestion to his own advantage. The elevation of an eyebrow. "I'm happy Kitten didn't have to come to that." His smile on Gratia was gentle. "Do whatever you wish tonight. But rest." He waited for her to respond but she was numb, half hidden behind the screen of Les Augustin. Let it go for tonight; tomorrow he would have her in his hands again. Now that this was over, he could really begin to mold her to that magnificence she promised. *The last act crowns the play.*

His exit was unhurried. But in the corridor again, the line echoing in his mind, he wondered. Les Augustin hadn't meant the curtain had fallen on the last act. He meant it was yet to come.

He softened his face quickly as a door opened on him. It was an elderly man and his wife; the cloak of security of position, mind and heart, tailored to them. It could never have been otherwise for them. For that one moment Viv stretched out his hands to their small respectability. He said, "Good evening."

"Good evening," the old man bowed. His wife smiled. She didn't know who he was but she knew he was important. When she read the Chicago papers tomorrow she would remember this brief meeting. She would feel pity for him, realizing how he'd hidden his grief under courtesy.

He remembered to walk slowly, his head bent, until he was within his room.

Mike's eyes lifted fearfully to his face. He smiled; he kept her waiting until he was seated, in punishment for her doubt. He said then, "Everything's all right. How about some dinner?"

She shook her head dumbly.

The train was slowing again, the whistles hooting their mournful signals. Nine-thirty-five, Dodge City. Change to Central time. It was as well he hadn't waited until after Dodge City. He wouldn't have had appetite for dinner if the ordeal had been hanging over him. He'd always had a nervous stomach. It was over; now he could enjoy a meal.

SEVEN

HE HAD TO GET the taste of Spender out of his mouth. He poured a double straight. Whatever he drank now wouldn't warm him. He was washed in the icy water of just rage.

He had known it was to happen and he hadn't prevented it. Even now he didn't know how he could have prevented it.

Gratia's voice was tremulous. "He didn't kill her. He didn't. Did he?"

"Yes, he killed her." Les spoke as to a child.

The drink stayed down. Hank said it again, pounding his frustration against the accomplished fact. "I shouldn't have let her go. I should have kept her away from him."

"What good would it have done?" Les's shrug was regretful. "He's good at murder. He killed his wife, you know."

Hank's voice was deceptively quiet. "I didn't know. You didn't tell me that." He began to curse. He saw Gratia's shocked face but he didn't care. He knew it wouldn't have changed things if he had known. But the bitterness within him had to be wreaked in violence.

Les understood. He said, "I didn't have a chance to tell you. Maybe I didn't quite believe it. Mike knows it was murder. She knows this is murder."

Sidney Pringle droned, "I thought she was sorry she didn't speak to me. I thought she was being kind to me. But it was because she was afraid, afraid to be alone. It was after he left her room." His breath quivered. "She was kind. She wanted to help me get started again." He sat very still and a hard shell formed on his sadness. "Why did he go to her room this morning? What did he do there?"

It was taking shape, fiercely Hank forced it to take shape. He hadn't saved Kitten; he would avenge her. Murder must be avenged. Between them, what they knew, each one his little knowledge, Viv Spender would face justice. Maybe it wouldn't hold up in court. It didn't need to. Spender might not pay with his eye and his tooth for hers; but he'd pay with living death, he'd pay in revulsion of human hearts, and after revulsion, oblivion. This case would be tried in the newspapers; Hank could attend to that.

Les read his silence, "It's no good. He did it the safe way."

"It's going to be good." Hank said, "He isn't going to get away with it. We know enough. Together we know enough."

Sidney Pringle said to himself, "She knew I was hungry. She had been hungry herself. She knew how it was. She paid for my lunch." His eyes filled with little flecks of fear. "She signed the check. Maybe he won't honor it now." He shook his head. "He couldn't be that niggardly. Not with her dead."

No one paid any attention to him.

Hank said, "Cobbett was out there all afternoon."

He acted. He swung open the door, called the name.

James Cobbett came out of compartment E. He held a pillow in one hand, a pillowcase in the other.

Hank said, "Come inside." Cobbett was hesitant. He'd had enough of them, those who had been a part of Kitten's last journey. He couldn't escape that easily; he too was a part of it.

He followed because he hated to pretend that Hank's need

was a Pullman duty, although he knew it concerned Kitten's death. He kept his hands busy with the pillow as he stood there waiting for Hank to make a request.

Hank asked it bluntly. "Did anyone go to Kitten Agnew's drawing room this afternoon? I mean after she went there, after she left Vivien Spender's room."

Cobbett shook his head.

Les said, "I told you it's no good, Hank. He's careful."

Hank refused defeat. He demanded recklessly, "Do you think Kitten Agnew died of heart trouble?"

He had no business asking it of James Cobbett; Cobbett had no business answering. Not answering as he did.

"I don't know about that. But I know she was sick when she came out of Mr. Spender's room. Dying." He feared death, or the way Kitten had to die. "I should have called the doctor then. But I didn't recognize it, and she didn't ask for help."

Cobbett spoke sadly. Remorse narrowed his face. Hank told him, "Don't blame yourself. I was beside her and I didn't know." His mind clutched tightly the bit of mosaic Cobbett had contributed. The deed had been done before she left Spender's room. The deed had been done in Hank's presence.

What had he been doing? Trying to anaesthetize his spirit. If he hadn't taken a drink, if he'd stopped at just one? He knew it would have made no difference. Kitten had only one cocktail, the lethal dose was in that one.

Cobbett shook the pillow into shape. "You should eat something." He was fatherly; he wanted to help their despair. "I can send Ben in when he comes to take Mr. Spender's order."

Gratia whispered, "I couldn't eat." Sidney Pringle swallowed saliva.

"Yes, send him in," Hank said. He wasn't thinking about it. There was something important to do, something more important than dinner. "The cocktail glasses. What happened to them? The glass she drank from?"

Cobbett said, "I don't know if Charles has taken the tray yet." He didn't say, you thought of it too late. A murderer wouldn't leave a glass to damn him. Hank was riddled with memory. It was the poison cup that had been smashed. Spender had made certain it was smashed.

He caught Cobbett's arm. "Broken. Pieces of glass."

Cobbett said, "There was glass on the floor when we met in Mr. Spender's room to decide what should be done. I swept it up."

Hank asked, "What happens to the sweepings?" He was holding it tight, clenching it, a scrap of hope.

"It's in the trash," Cobbett said, "It won't be taken off until Chicago." It didn't matter if Cobbett believed; he understood. "Small pieces only, splinters."

"Even a splinter." The detection of modern scientific laboratories. He wondered who was yet in homicide that he had known. What police reporters were on the dailies. The same old legs?

Cobbett said, "I must finish the Shellabargers' berths. They want to get to bed early." It was an excuse, to get away. He went away.

Les said, "The Shellabargers." If he laughed, he would cough and he mustn't cough. But it was too funny to pass. His mouth tweaked. "The Shellabargers have had such a lovely trip. Rather dull, of course."

Hank growled, "For God's sake, Les." But he was secretly exultant. Les was himself again. He needed Les to finish this. Not a Les gauzed within a strange dream. The monkey Les, biting, scratching, gibbering.

Les said, "I'd rather be a Shellabarger. I shudder to think

about tomorrow. Questions bore me. When the other fellow asks them."

Sidney Pringle gnawed his finger. "Questions?" His voice squeaked.

Pringle quivered anxiously, "I have nothing to say, I won't say Vivien Spender is a murderer. I don't think he is. A man like Vivien Spender wouldn't kill." He was running away now, as fast as his spindle legs could carry him. Before it had begun, he fled. He wouldn't stand up to Spender power, no matter how he wanted Spender to grovel in the dust. He was conditioned to the strong grinding the weak, the rich battering the poor. Until the poor and the weak became the rich and the strong, he wouldn't fight openly. He wouldn't chance Spender's disapproval; he was too certain. Spender would come out whole. Only an heroic fool risked his own skin throwing in his lot with a lost cause. Smart, he would call himself.

This miserable, stinking wretch; this porous, articulate lower animal form. Who was there to say that Pringle's clay was not set here only to hold the mirror of self-portraiture to Hank Cavanaugh? To the cowardice of Hank Cavanaugh who had run out on a lost cause.

Hank's upper lip curled. "You'll tell the truth or you'll go to jail for perjury. Whatever Spender pays you to be on his side."

Pringle's mouth was secret. That hadn't occurred to him yet, the gratefulness of Spender. Grateful to his friends, even his unknown friends. The reward.

Hank was savage. "You'll testify the right way at the inquest or you'll—"

Pringle jumped out of his fantasy, back into the grimness of his reality. "An inquest? We'll have to stay in Chicago for an inquest?" He shook his head. "I can't do it."

"Are you in that big a hurry for the necktie counter?" Hank

was deliberately cruel. "Are you in that big a rush to go back to nothing?"

Pringle said, "I have no place to stay in Chicago. At least in New York I can sleep in my father's apartment. It's three flights up over a delicatessen." He flagellated himself before these betters out of habit. "It smells of pickles and at night the rats gnaw at the boxes." He bit his finger. That too was habit because he wasn't sorrowing now; he was dreaming of his name coupled with the names of the great, Kitten Agnew, Vivien Spender, Leslie Augustin. He'd duck and feint but he wouldn't run so far that his name wasn't in the papers.

Les said, "Don't feed him out of your plate, Hank. He might turn into an orchestra leader."

Pringle complained, "I'm a writer. I don't want to be an orchestra leader."

Gratia's eyes were made of glass, dark glass. You could see through them to the bottomless depth of her, but it was too dark to know what you saw there. She turned them on Les. Her throat was sore. "Why did he want to kill Kitten?"

Les said, "Darling," and the word was honey on his tongue as it had been last night. But he had no other words for her. He was saved by Ben at the door.

"Want to order your dinner now, Mr. Augustin?"

Les said, "We do, Ben." He asked softly, "What is Mr. Spender eating tonight?"

Ben was fat and smooth as coffee cream. He was professional in pride and he didn't even know that Kitten was said to be ill. He grinned. "The steak dinner. It's the best."

Silence crackled louder than the rush of the train.

Les pricked the order. "Bring us four steak dinners. We too want only the best."

Ben bowed his bulk out, he was whistling as he closed the door on them.

Les said mildly, "May he have good appetite."

Gratia's voice cut like a knife. "Why did he kill Kitten?"

"Because—" If he didn't look at her, if he clattered the words, Hank could say them. "Because he wanted you in her place."

The Chief cantered on into the cold night.

—2—

Mike sat alone in her tiny walled cell. Until the metronome of the train's wheels rose to crescendo, until the wail of the train whistle across the flatlands had crushed her heart to pulp. Wondering at the loneliness of the new dead, remembering Kitten and Kitten's need for light and life. She had no sorrow for Kitten dead; she had pity that scalded.

She couldn't endure her own loneness longer. She must look on a human face, must know that she was still among the living.

She didn't dare go to the club car. She couldn't conceal her agony from those who would be watching her, watching Viv Spender's secretary. They would know at once something was wrong; gossip writers' intuition was developed to the soundness of knowledge. She couldn't go to him; she no longer could play a part before him. If she went, she must accuse.

She hadn't known with Althea. She'd only feared it had been he. No one else had been suspicious of him. Not at that time. How could she alone accuse? Yet she had known, known out of her knowledge of him and of Althea, known and remained silent.

There was no doubt in her mind this time. She had knowledge of what he was. She had knowledge when his head fell on Kitten's breast. He was a murderer.

She had led him away because it was expected of her, because he expected it. With the dull mobility of a drugged person, she had remained with him until the ordeal was over, until with genial expansiveness he discussed dinner with Ben. She fled then, fled from the honor of this evil being who had taken possession of the man she had known as Viv Spender.

She didn't want to return to him. Yet she knew she must. She must return and accuse him. Her heart was ragged in her breast. Not because she feared for herself; because she feared for him; she didn't know what was to become of him.

With even steps, Mike walked out of the narrow room. It took all of her strength to open the vestibule door. The biting cold air scratched her lungs. There was no indecision as she pushed into the dim corridor of the death car. She felt her way past the door of Kitten's room, loath to continue forward but impelled. Past doors of honest people, to Les Augustin's door.

Why couldn't Les have been the one who killed Kitten? Les who had come to her last night, prying out the story of the first Mrs. Spender's death. It could have been Les. Or Hank Cavanaugh or Sidney Pringle. Even Gratia Shawn. All had opportunity. It had been Viv Spender's hand. The others hadn't ordered a sleeping draught in Kitten's name.

She didn't stop at Les's door. She slowed but her steps moved on. She stopped at Viv's room because that was the end of the corridor. She couldn't enter. No place to go now but back to the cell, to sit alone with the nightmare. She realized suddenly that she was not alone. James Cobbett had come around the corner, from the linen closet. He was standing there looking down at her.

He looked at her with the objectivity of a judge on the bench. He was like Viv Spender in a strange way, a handsome figure of a man, tall, commanding. The likeness was surface. This man was honest, it was his solid core. And he was kind, despite the cruelty he must have known, he was not embittered. He suffered with the suffering, he suffered with her now although he could not know the reason for her anguish. He was the man Viv Spender should have been, if Viv had not become warped by his power.

Her knees buckled and she laid her hand against the cold metal wall for support. He said, "Can I help you, Ma'm?"

He could help her. He could tell her what to do. She shook her head. "No." She turned and started slowly to retrace her path back to herself.

She was halted by the opening of a door. A big waiter was backing out, balancing a loaded tray. She hadn't noticed the door; she didn't know she was visible until she heard the voice, the rapier voice pricking her name.

"Mike. Come in. We've been waiting for you to come."

Without volition yet almost with relief she walked inside.

The four of them looked steadily at her as they had done earlier. She met Les's eyes. And she saw that now they were not hostile, they were merciless. The sigh curled from her mouth.

"What are you going to do?"

She asked, "What are you going to do?" but she knew without asking. There had been no softening in any of them during the period when she had sat alone in her emptiness. They did not answer her question. They looked at her; they watched her falter into the chair, not because she wanted to remain with them, because her legs would no longer support the weight she carried.

It was Les who answered her. Gentle as a sigh. "We're going to hang Vivien Spender."

He need not have answered; she knew before he spoke. She said, "You can't do that."

They didn't understand, they scorned her doubt.

He said, "We believe that we can." He rested his fair head against his clasped hands. "We must think of Hank's career. He's been away a long time, he needs some stories. There's a good one

I heard about Vivien Spender a long time ago. When there was a Mrs. Spender. I have friends who must remember Mrs. Spender. I think they will remember quite a bit about her."

"It'll make a good Sunday feature." Hank Cavanaugh's mouth was brutal. "The tragic deaths of the two women loved by Viv Spender. 'For each man kills the thing he loves—'"

"Not a bald statement Hank," Les purred. "Let's not be crude. The merest suggestion will start speculation."

"We'll do a little speculating to the Chicago police tomorrow. There's a guy I used to know—he ought to be a captain or something by now. Homicide. A big case could make his name. A smart guy. Bulldog, we used to call him. Liked to get his teeth into a case—"

She said again, "You can't do it," and again they misunderstood.

Les said, "There's another story in the tragedy that has dogged the footsteps of those nominated to play Clavdia Chauchat. Sob stuff. A touch of the mysterious. Will Clavdia Chauchat ever be seen on the screen?" He shook his head in mock regret. "Not under Viv Spender's direction."

Hank said, "Then there's the story of Kitten Agnew. That's a feature all to itself. It's surefire. Maybe it'll be dynamite. If her lawyer wants to talk." Les smiled. "I think he'll talk. I think he'll give an interview that will be front-page material. Then Pringle here—"

Pringle said, "I don't know anything. I can't help you."

Les's smile sharpened. "Pringle heard so many rumors on the lot. He had no friends there; no one to talk with so he listened. He heard plenty of Spender's plans—"

It hadn't been that way when New Essany was new. There'd been a personal loyalty then to the Boss. Spender wasn't so far away then; he was one among his workers he was one of them. He'd become too big.

"And that brings us to Gratia Shawn." Les's lips were a scimitar. "The new Clavdia Chauchat."

The girl was colorless. "I didn't know. I didn't want to take her place. I wouldn't try to take anyone's place."

Hank said, "We have Gratia's contract. He never intended to let Kitten's case come into court. He couldn't win it. You won't deny that. He couldn't make Gratia a star when he was in prison. He had to get rid of Kitten."

"You have no proof," Mike told him.

"That's proof enough. Put it all together, it's proof enough."

She shook her head. This time she said it right. "You can't do it to him. He's not like other men."

Pringle's round little mouth quivered. "He's no better than we are. Money doesn't make a man better."

"I didn't say he was better," she said quietly. "I said he wasn't like other men. He isn't."

Gratia's hands were a white stain on the black stuff of her dress. "He isn't sane. He can't have been sane."

Les said, "He's as sane as you or I." He took a small breath. "With one small exception. He thinks he's Almighty God."

Four of them. Four strangers. They would avenge Kitten. She had meant little to them living; she meant little more dead. It was not Kitten, it was murder they would avenge.

It was Cavanaugh who held them together. Because he was a crusader. Because his craw was overfed with death.

Without him, the others would be without strength. Gratia was too muted with horror to act. Sidney Pringle was afraid to take sides; his slack jowls wobbled as he balanced on the fence. He hated the great man but he feared to speak. Les Augustin played the wasp but he hadn't the energy for active hate. He would demolish only if it could be accomplished without soiling his nails.

Yet in Cavanaugh's strength the four were as one, determined to destroy Viv Spender. They faced her with their unmoving, un-flickering eyes. They did not know that she had come because she too knew he must be destroyed. What little remained of him not already destroyed by pride and self-will. She had not been sure of it herself until now. She differed from these four in one respect alone; she would be merciful. She had said the truth; he was not as other men. In his mind he believed his act was right. He had rid himself of a disease that threatened his existence.

Because he was valuable, he must protect himself. There was no wrong in self-protection. He was as sane as any other man, save for one thing.

Strength was returning to her. She must have strength for what she was to do. Not because she condoned. Because despite the sins, and his were heavy, love was changeless. It was hers to do, not these strangers with their varying motives. Because she had been weak before, and by her weakness had allowed his guilt to mount, she must be strong now.

They waited for her to speak. They must believe she stood by him. They must not know she meant to cheat them of their triumph. She said, "You have no proof."

Hank answered her. "We will have after the autopsy."

"What if you do find poison?" she demanded. "You can't prove he gave it to her."

Hank smiled. "We have the glass she drank from."

"It was broken," she said quickly.

"Even broken glass can be tested."

She could tell them about the bottle she'd come on in Viv's desk. A small bottle. Prescribed for in Kitten's name. She could tell her horror and her sickness as she closed it away in the drawer. Because she knew Kitten had not ordered it. For months he had refused to see Kitten. Because she had seen a similar bottle once before, on the bed table of a young woman who died too soon.

She said nothing. They would not need the information. She would not betray him to these who hated him. She would go to him now. If they would let her go. As she rose their eyes rustled suspicion.

It was Les who quelled them. "It doesn't matter if he knows. There's nothing he can do now."

She said, "He wouldn't believe me if I told him."

Les smiled, "If he asks why, tell him we're afraid murder might become a habit with him. He mustn't be allowed to do it again."

They didn't stop her as she left the room. They believed there was nothing he could do now.

—3—

Sidney Pringle began to shake as with a chill. His words stammered. "I'm not a drinking man. Could I have a little drink now? I'm cold, so cold."

"You're afraid," Leslie Augustin said. He didn't open his eyes to speak. His head was against the back of the seat. The life was drained out of him, under his tan you could see the pallor. His tongue scorned softly, "You're afraid."

Pringle took the glass that Cavanaugh, wordless, held out. He drank one inch of the whiskey, finished the second inch but it didn't help. He said, "Yes, I'm afraid. Aren't the rest of you afraid?"

There wasn't an answer. Cavanaugh poured himself a drink and drank it. Les Augustin was stretched motionless across the seat. Gratia sat in blurred silence by the window.

He tried to tell them. "You don't know what he is. We can't do anything to him. He's too powerful. He'll get out of it. We won't be safe ever again." They didn't hear him. "You don't know what he can do to us."

Augustin said, "I know." He opened his tired eyes and there were pinpoints of excitement stabbing the pupils. "I know. I've fought him for a long time. Now I want to end it."

Cavanaugh put down his glass. He was curious. "Why have you fought him, Les? What did he ever do to you?"

"I don't know." Distaste sloped his shoulders. "I never liked him."

"That's no excuse."

"I think it is. Something tells you not to like certain persons. Not why. Sometimes you learn why later. Sometimes you don't."

Cavanaugh hung his legs over the arm of the chair. "You learned why this time." It wasn't a question.

"Yes. Gratia."

She hadn't spoken for a long time. She'd said now, "You didn't see me until yesterday. You didn't know I existed."

Augustin went on in that fine, silken-thread voice. "Something inside of me knew there'd be a Gratia someday and knew what he'd do to her. I've been trying to stop him all these years." He moved his slender eyes to Pringle's face. "Yes, I'm afraid. I've always been afraid of him. Afraid I couldn't stop him in time. I'm not afraid any more. Not of him."

Gratia said again, "You didn't know me. I couldn't have anything to do with you and Viv Spender."

"You did." Augustin's fingers threaded together.

Cavanaugh shook his head, "I don't know. I don't know you, Les. I've never known you."

"No one has ever known me," Augustin said pleasantly. "I've never let anyone know me. Because I was afraid." He turned to Pringle and he shuddered delicately. "He says he's afraid. The rest of us wouldn't say so. We're too civilized. But we're afraid all the time."

Pringle said, "You're making fun of me. Because I'm afraid of what you're planning to do tomorrow."

Augustin looked at Cavanaugh. "I've been afraid of being hurt. All my life. Everything I've done has been to keep myself from being hurt. What I am is out of fear." He mused. "If it weren't for being afraid, I'd be a concert violinist. Starving for the purity of my art." He juggled the idea. "One of the fiddle section of the Philharmonic. On the side giving lessons to little boys, nasty little boys whose mothers dream for them to be in the fiddle section someday. And give lessons to—"

Hank Cavanaugh had been thinking of fear today, but he hadn't been thinking deep enough. Now it was said. "Maybe it's fear that makes all of us tick. Maybe you're right." He worried his forehead. "Kitten was afraid to die. I'm not afraid of that. I wonder if Viv Spender is afraid of that." He denied it. "No, he's not afraid of anything. That's why he's a monster. He isn't human. That's why we can plan his destruction, Pringle. We know he's extinct."

Pringle insisted hoarsely. "You don't know how powerful he is. With his lawyers and investigators and bankers—all his money. He'll beat us. We can't help but lose."

"We won't lose." Cavanaugh's smile was cold iron. "We haven't anything to lose. There's nothing he can take away from any of us. We haven't anything."

"Our futures," Pringle whimpered.

Cavanaugh's voice threatened. "Nobody can take away your future. Nobody can take away something you don't have yet. When you get it, it's up to you what you do with it."

"Bravo." Les's eyebrows winged. Surprise had tilted his voice. "You're all right now, aren't you, Hank?"

Cavanaugh's hand went across his face. "Maybe I am," he said. "I hope I am." He was feeling his way through a miasma of muddled thought. "I don't know. I've been afraid too. Afraid of all the evil, afraid there wasn't any good left." He looked at Gratia; she might have slept, her lashes lay heavy on her cheeks.

"There is good. That's what we keep searching for. All our lives. Most of us don't find it. Don't know how to find it."

Pringle complained, "I don't know what you're talking about. You won't listen to me. I'm trying to tell you about him."

Cavanaugh said to Les Augustin, "Good can be untouched by evil. If it is truly good."

He looked again at her and her eyes lifted to his. As if she understood all the half-words he had spoken.

But she said, "I'm afraid too. Nothing will ever be the same again."

She brushed her hair away from her face. "I didn't want Kitten's part or Kitten's life. I didn't understand how it was. You called me innocent, Hank. It wasn't innocence, it was ignorance. Because I'd never had to fight. I never knew what it meant to fight for your very existence."

He looked again into her face. And he saw it was blemished with the beginning of knowledge. She had spoken truly. She had never had to fight for the existence of self. The fight that must be fought. Even when blood came from your mouth, even when you had lost all vestiges of pride, even when you lifted your head and went out clutching the rag of fear. Even when victory was descent again into the bowels of hell. It was this fight which made the incongruous three, he, Les Augustin, Pringle, one with Kitten. Gratia had been too young, too untouched, too lucky to know what desperation bound them together.

He said to her, "No, it won't be the same again. The fairy prince, the marble palace—"

She shook her head gently. "They wouldn't be enough now. Now that I'm awake."

If there were a world somewhere without evil, if he and Gratia could come together there, it would be good. He had nothing to offer her in this world but his own dark anguish. Even she could not bring him peace. He had to go back, he'd known it all along; he couldn't run far enough away. He had to return from whence he fled. Peace wasn't for him, not until the last mouth had been fed.

He said, "I had a dream too." With the decision made, the burden was lightened. He could breathe.

Les said lightly,

"It is not, Celia, in our power
To say how long our love will last . . ."

He was holding her beauty in his eyes, drinking it into memory. He didn't know his heart was also in his eyes; he hadn't had experience with love. "I tire easily," he said. "I'd even tire of the good and beautiful." He knew he mustn't cough but he brought forth his thin golden cigarette case. The insouciant gesture for the lie. "I tire of all but the great Augustin."

Hank pulled the cigarette from his fingers. "It's no good, Les." The cynic with the rosebud-wreathed heart. "You didn't get it. I'm going back."

Les shook his head slowly. "You can't do that. You can't leave Gratia to the jackals. Once Spender is gone, they'll be baying on her heels."

Hank grinned, "She'll have you." He wasn't afraid to turn her over to Les now. Les cared enough to want to give her up. Enough to lie for her sake.

She broke in hotly. "You can't dispose of me that way. I'm not a cotton-wool toy any longer. I'm awake." She drew a tremulous breath. "You've watched over me all the journey. You held my hand as if I were a little child, you didn't let me wander off alone, you didn't let me see anything ugly. You wanted me to stay enchanted in my ignorance."

Hank said honestly, "We needed you the way you were."

She made a quick gesture. "Don't think I'm not appreciative. You were good, so good, both of you. You didn't want me hurt by what was going to happen. You didn't want me shamed by finding out." She wasn't regretful. "I had to know. I had to be shamed. Now I'll learn. What all of you have always known. The way to fight for what you want to come true. Dreaming isn't enough; you have to fight."

Les whispered, "Darling." It wasn't an interruption.

She said, "Maybe someday I will play Clavdia. After I've learned."

Hank beetled at Les. "Maybe caviar three times a day won't be as tasty now, Augustin. Now you've something better to live for." His eyes moved to Gratia. "When it comes to fighting Les is a good teacher."

Pringle fretted. "None of you understand." He trembled with frustration.

Les pitied. "You're the one who doesn't understand. You're still thinking of neckties. We're pricking our fingers on stars."

—4—

James Cobbett sat in the dull-lit corridor on the small seat under the frame of his name card. He sat there heavy-eyed watching three doors. Three rooms not yet made up for the night although the hour had passed midnight. One door behind which no bell could ring. Two doors where he dare not knock and request they go to bed.

The old couple in E were asleep long ago. Knowing nothing of death riding with them. The young couple in C were moon-wandering. Not dreaming of the extra passenger that had, unknown, ridden the Chief. He had ached to warn Debby and Fred Crandall as he spoke his sober, "Good night." Don't be too happy. Be afraid to be too happy.

She must have been happy that way once. She must have loved and been loved. Because she had once been warm and young and alive. Now she was cold and still. Death didn't care

whether he chose young or old. He was a robot, touching who-
ever lay in his path. Death didn't belong on board the Chief. It
belonged in dark hallways. Death shouldn't have been stalking
someone made of shimmering life, someone shining like Kitten
Agnew.

James Cobbett was afraid sitting there, urging the train forward, knowing it was of no avail, the length of the journey was
inexorably bound. He would not be home until tomorrow. He
would not touch Mary until tomorrow, know she was safe, and
the children.

He was afraid because his thumbs were not quieted. What
had hung over this journey had not been vanquished by Kitten
Agnew's death. Maybe if those who knew her would weep, this
haunt would be washed away. They weren't weeping. They were
closeted together with the *judge ye* a flint in their fists. Judgment,
without mercy, in their knotted fists.

Three rooms. In the far room the clay of Kitten Agnew, un-
tenanted. In the near room Vivien Spender, the man who had
been her creator, the man who had wept briefly; the man they
accused of murder. In the mid-room the accusers.

The lovely girl who had been quiet before Kitten's glitter,
more quiet now that the light was put out. The cheap little man
who had been moist-eyed when Kitten lived, whose eyes were
dried to black buttons. The angular man who had been drunk
last night and into this day; who was brutally sober tonight despite the bottle under his hand, Augustin whose languor had
become nerves. The efficient secretary who moved now like a
sleep-walker.

The Chief panted across the dark coldness of the Kansas
prairie. Cobbett sat there dozing, thinking long thoughts, dozing
again. He woke to the sound of a door opening. The mid-room.
Ready for bed at last. But only one person came from it. It was

the secretary. She wasn't walking in her sleep now. Her face had grown old, but it was calm. Her movement was steady. If she saw James Cobbett, she gave no sign. She moved to the door of Vivien Spender's room. She didn't knock. She opened it and went inside. His fear was greater than before.

—5—

When he heard the door open, he lifted his head in surprise. It was entirely unexpected that the door should open at this hour. It was only natural that he would turn quickly to see who was entering. Nothing to do with nerves, his were as easy as a mill pond on a summer afternoon.

He saw Mike. He shouldn't have been struck by a second dart of surprise, who else would come to him but Mike? Yet he was surprised. Because he had believed when she left earlier that she wouldn't face him again until it could be amidst the confusion of strangers tomorrow. Mike was afraid he had killed Kitten.

She had been afraid. She wasn't now. She came in and closed the door and she stood there as impersonal as if she'd come from the next office at his summons. He was relieved and secretly triumphant that she had come to her senses. Not that he hadn't expected her to return to them. Her few lapses from the unemotional, competent Mike Dana, secretary, had been rare over their years, together. But he felt relief that she had reverted to her norm without the need of his intervention. The secret triumph was male; he had reconquered Mike and his pride was bulbous.

He hid all this. He asked her kindly, with a small, proper seasoning of surprise, "What's the matter, Mike? Why aren't you in bed?"

She said, "I've been with Les Augustin."

His hands pressed down flat on the table. She didn't know

the weight of their pressure; she didn't know that the anchored table would have splintered if it had been wood not metal. She continued with the relentless impersonality.

"And Hank Cavanaugh. And Sidney Pringle. And Gratia Shawn."

The suffusion of anger was hot in his face. He had forgotten. He hadn't even remembered the time, he was still dressed at this hour because he'd forgotten everything in his work. It was here on paper, the idea by which Gratia Shawn would be introduced. Here was the first rung of the starry ladder which would in time lead her up to the part of Clavdia Chauchat. He'd blocked out scenes, he'd synopsized an idea to be turned over to his highest-priced writers for development. Something simple and good, yet strong; something like Gratia herself. In his concentration, he had forgotten. As he could always forget in his work. What had been done this day was over with; he and time had passed beyond it, as irrevocably as the Chief had passed beyond La Junta and Dodge City.

He was angry that Mike should remember what had gone by. He had believed she too had forgotten; not that she had been diddering over the past with Les Augustin. However, he was careful to speak not in anger but in exasperation. "For God's sake, why? I saw them earlier. I told you everything was all right." He knew how to make his smile boyish, excited. He knew the answering smile of enthusiasm she would give in turn. "I've been sitting here planning the first picture for Gratia. I'll open it—"

She broke in. Her voice was level. "Everything isn't all right, Viv."

The performance was ended. There was a brackish taste in his mouth. "What do you mean?"

"Tomorrow they will accuse you of the murder of Kitten."

For a long moment they watched each other. Then he laughed. It had never come so hard. Because this woman knew him as he would know himself if he dared. Because she had not forgotten the past or any of the Vivien Spenders of the past, and no matter how excellent a performance he could give before her, she would not forget. She was his conscience. The idea fleeted across his mind and he marked it for future use. A living separate conscience pursuing a character. But he was stronger than conscience. He'd recognized her for what she was long before this night. He had conquered her, ruled her. Unless a man could conquer and rule that atavistic impulse called conscience, it would become a Cassandraic nuisance.

For the long moment they watched each other—then he tossed back his head and laughed. "That's the silliest thing I've ever heard of."

There was no reaction in her to his laughter or to what he had said. She was looking at him as if he were a stranger. She said at last, "No, Viv."

It was difficult to control his anger in the face of her imperturbable negation. She knew better than to goad him this way. She knew how to protect him from his fury. Yet she said, "No, Viv," and there was no more feeling in her face than in a face of stone. She sat down on the chair. And she said without feeling, "They know you murdered her."

"They don't know anything." His mouth was brutal. He saw the shape of it in the mirror and she saw it because she was looking at him. But she wasn't afraid.

"They know you murdered her. They are prepared to prove it."

"They can't prove anything of the kind." He never shouted, he wasn't shouting now. He was holding his voice so tight that his throat muscles ached. He began to laugh again. This time he was truly laughing, "You must be crazy letting a bunch of drunks upset you this way. You're worn out, Mike. After we wash up this premiere you must take a real vacation. It's been years since you've had a decent one."

She said in that same level drone, "They are going to the police in Chicago tomorrow. And to the newspapers."

He kept on laughing. "Do you think any sane person would listen to such a ridiculous accusation against me?" He was Vivien Spender; had she forgotten? "As for the newspapers—" His laughter heightened, then he broke it and looked at her shrewdly. "There are libel laws. Come, Mike. Let's have a nightcap and then you get to bed. Tomorrow you'll realize how absurd this is."

He pushed away from the table and he walked over to the tray stand near her chair. She watched him out of steady eyes.

"Unless you're afraid to drink with me."

She watched his hands pouring the drinks. She said, "I'm not afraid to drink with you. You can't get rid of all of us."

He said, "No one credits Augustin. He's a malicious gossip. Pringle's a disgruntled writer that we fired. Cavanaugh's an alcoholic. Gratia—" He smiled. "She's an impressionable child. Tomorrow I'll talk to her." He shot seltzer into the glasses. "Are you one with them, Mike?"

She said, "There was a bottle in your desk. Of sleeping tablets."

He was calm again. As calm as she. He asked, "You saw it in my desk?"

"Yes."

"You didn't mention it."

"No." The hesitation was so slight he might not have noticed if all sound had not been heightened by that fraction of silence. "Because I knew when I saw it. With her name on it." Again there was the infinitesimal moment of silence. "I hoped terribly that I was wrong." She was as stone but her voice was scalded with tears.

She went on, "There are pieces of broken glass. The glass she drank from."

His back was to her; she couldn't see this new anger mottling his face. She was lying. They'd lied to her. No one on the Chief would have saved that broken glass. They'd sent her to try to frighten him. He finished stirring the drinks, passed one to her. He had the glass to his lips when she spoke again.

"They know about Althea's death."

He didn't taste, he put down the glass. A spill of it fell across the scrawled white paper. He took his handkerchief from his pocket and blotted the liquid from the paper. He spoke the name without meaning. "Althea?"

She said, "I told them you killed her."

How could she remember that far away? He'd forgotten years ago. Althea was no more real to him than a character he'd written into a picture and later cut away. He couldn't remember the shape of her or the color of her hair or the way she had spoken.

Why had Mike kept silent all these years if she remembered Althea? Why had she waited until this moment of pinnacle to speak? He looked at her and his voice was parched. "How you must hate me."

"No," she said. "I love you. I've always loved you." She came quietly across the small room, carrying her drink. She set it on the table beside his glass. She slid into the seat directly across from him.

She said, "I can't bear to have you suffer. The way they plan for you to suffer. They intend to crucify you, Viv. For what you did to Kitten." She took her glass but she didn't drink; she held it quiet in her hand.

What did Kitten mean to them? He knew before he planned this that there would be no one to regret her removal. She had no friends. Why should these strangers care what had happened to her?

He asked it. "Why?"

She said slowly, "I don't think you can understand. I don't

think I can explain it myself. It's different with each one of them. But it's the same. It's a question of right and wrong."

He was sardonic. "Perhaps I can understand better than you think. Perhaps they are the ones who can't understand. My right and wrong may be bigger than theirs." His head was clearing. "What I don't understand is how they turned you against me. I won't ever understand that."

She smiled at him and her smile was sadder than the anguish of tears. "I remember the first time I saw you. You didn't have anything. I remember your shirt, it was a blue shirt. You wore blue shirts because they didn't show wear so quickly. You had your hair cut very short—it didn't need to be cut so often. But you had pride and faith. You were on fire with ambition. I knew you were destined for greatness."

She was forcing him to remember. He had known too, known he was going to reach greatness. He hadn't become great by weakness. You couldn't become great if you were soft. You had to be strong enough to force the unyielding pattern.

She said, "I've walked with you every step of the way. It wasn't easy at first. There were nothing but dreams of someday. Do you remember when you lived on those dreams, Viv?" She took a slow breath. "I loved you. You never loved me; you took me, yes, but you didn't love me. That didn't matter. It has never mattered. As long as I could be beside you."

He'd never loved her, no. He loved beauty and she was plain. Yet she had meant more to him than any he had loved. He had been willing always to do without them but never without Mike. She was his flaw, his weakness. If he'd got rid of her long ago, when he first realized she knew him too well, she wouldn't have been here to condemn him tonight. To hand him over to his motley judges. He hadn't rid himself of her because he had believed he needed her, because he hadn't been able to see his way without Mike.

She said, "I thought I'd lose you when those dreams became actuality. I didn't. I learned how to keep you. By living only through you. It was enough."

If she were gone, he could handle the others. They were weaklings, all of them. Money was all he needed to take care of them; he had plenty of money. Mike was their strength, without her word and knowledge, the little four had nothing.

She said, "It would still be enough for me, Viv. Even now when you've failed."

"Failed?" The word was whiplash and he started from its thong.

"Yes, failed." That sad smile was across her eyes. "No one else knows yet. The first thing you lost was ambition. You traded the dream of your masterpiece for cheap affairs. The Viv Spender I first knew wouldn't have done that."

She didn't understand, she couldn't understand a man's search for perfection. He took up his highball and drank from it. Perhaps he had made some mistakes. Maybe he'd seen Clavdia Chauchat where she couldn't possibly be. He could be allowed a few errors. He hadn't made many.

"Faith? You lost your faith long ago. I don't know how it happened. Maybe too much money does that to a man. You stopped believing in yourself; you believed only in things. There's nothing left but your pride. I hope you haven't lost your pride." She was beginning to break, her voice caught for a moment. He barely heard the name. "Doumel."

He was shaken by rage. His tongue was thick. "I'm not a Doumel. That mangy French tomcat. I threw him off my lot."

Her words had a dreadful inevitability. "There was only one girl in the case of Doumel. She didn't die. It was unfortunate she was so young. Perhaps he didn't know any better, he hadn't been in this country for long. Do you remember the trial? The hideous long trial, the testimony in the newspapers? Do you remember his face when the sentence was pronounced? He's in prison now. He'll be there a long time. When he comes out, no one will remember him. He might as well be dead."

He drained his glass, set it down. She couldn't force him to listen any longer. He could silence her too.

She said, "He had dreams once. I wonder what he dreams of now." Her face had no expression. "Comfortable clothes? His car? Going into a restaurant and ordering whatever he wants? Or just of being free."

He knew the hideousness of men shut away from everything that made life decent. He had visited prisons before he made the first big picture of prison life. He remembered the dead face of one man who was shut in for life, a man who had killed his wife, a murderer. He wasn't a murderer! What he had done couldn't be called murder! It was justice.

He scoffed, "If you're afraid of ghosts, I'm not. Nor of Augustin and his friends. They can't do anything to me. When I get through with them, they'll be sorry they started anything."

There was pity in her, pity for him! A pity that was scorn. "You can't laugh off judgment day, Viv. It's been a long time coming but it's at hand now. You can face it any way you choose. I hoped you'd choose to face it proudly." Her mouth was stern. "This time you can't escape. You'll have to pay."

She believed her words. She expected him to believe. She'd forgotten that he was Vivien Spender. Pity and scorn, mockery and tears were for little men. For weak men. Not for Vivien Spender. He said, "If you're through, I'd like to tell you my plans. For Gratia." He paused to give her his smile.

She was unsmiling. "If you go in to Chicago tomorrow, you can't escape, Viv." Her breath came slowly. "That's why I had to turn against you. To save you. To let you die as you've lived, a great man. So that the legend of Viv Spender wouldn't die too."

She was dispassionate as stone. The monstrous horror of her

suggestion suddenly smote him. If her voice had trembled, if she'd been touched with tears, he wouldn't have believed. She was turned to stone. She meant he should end his life.

His eyes blurred with that horror. The police. They couldn't arrest him. They could hold him. They wouldn't dare. They would dare because they would call it murder. He couldn't make them understand; even Mike did not understand.

Panic stirred in him. If the police held him, if the poison was found both in the body and on the splintered glass, if the prescription was traced to him—men had been condemned to die on such stupid trifles. They couldn't put him to death! He faced the eternity of prison. The humiliation of being caged like an animal, of being demeaned to the stature of Doumel. If he were in time pardoned, to come broken into a hostile world. A world with no sympathy for failure. Too old to fight upward again. Kitten had pulled the pillars down about him. He was eaten by his fury but he could not vent it on her because she was dead. Dying she had destroyed him.

He wasn't destroyed! He wouldn't be destroyed. There was too much to live for. He had lawyers, he was Viv Spender. He was not to die.

His hand was shaking. He steadied it about the empty glass. He needed another drink. He needed to fix another for her. But there was a lethargy in him that kept him seated, listening to her lies.

"There is no choice," she said. "There is nothing left but death." Her voice was shattered. "The unknown is better than the known of living death."

He would fix the drink for her, force it down her lying throat. He started to rise, but he couldn't rise.

The cold of the glass sped through his fingers into his heart. Frantically he tried to recall. He hadn't been watching her; he didn't know what she had done to her glass. He hadn't seen the sleight of her hand when she took up his, left for him the one she had made lethal. She too had boarded the Chief with a vial of death.

The emptiness of the glass was heavy in his hand. It slipped away, but the sound it made falling was dull, muffled. Gratia . . . *Gratia!* That was the bitter cup, to have found Clavdia after long years of search, to have found her and lost her in the space of brief time. The dream would die with him. It would never be fulfilled because there would never be another Spender.

Mike's eyes were motionless on him, desert dry in her stone face.

His head drooped. Through his heavy lids he saw again a spill on the white paper. There would be no agony, only the anguish of his tortured heart crying out to live. He had too much pride to let Mike know. With painful slowness he took his handkerchief from his pocket. His hand crawled out to blot the stain . . .

—6—

She heard the slump. She didn't see because her eyes had been without focus since he had drained the glass she had placed for him. She had kept words moving, her apologia. It would be easier for him if he understood why.

She forced herself to look. The massive head was bowed over the table. She whispered, "Viv." The cry broke from her, "Viv!"

She could be silent now. Be silent and wait. Wait alone as she would always be alone now, the living death. The train clacked and whinnied through the long night into the bleak of dawn.

She could no longer hear his tired breath. She had killed him. She pushed out from the table. Her untouched glass she carried into the bathroom. She poured out the contents, rinsed it, dried it and placed it on the serving tray. She walked to the door and opened it.

James Cobbett was sitting patiently in his place. His eyes turned up to her. He might have been waiting all the night long for this.

She said quietly, "Will you call a doctor? Mr. Spender has had a heart attack."

The world would believe he died in grief. She waited there, watching as Cobbett swayed with the rushing train until he was out of sight. She went then to the door of Leslie Augustin's room. She opened it and stood in the doorway, harsh in her bitter triumph. The four were there, silenced, waiting. They looked up at her the same way James Cobbett had, as if they knew what she was about to say.

AMERICAN
MYSTERY *from*
CLASSICS

*Available now
in hardcover and paperback:*

AMERICAN MYSTERY CLASSICS

from

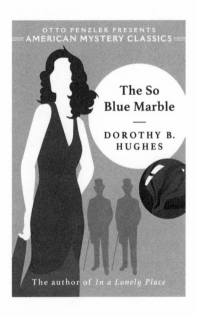

Want more **Dorothy B. Hughes**? Check out
the author's suspenseful debut novel,
The So Blue Marble,
out now in hardcover and paperback
from Penzler Publishers!

Read on for the terrifying first chapter...

I

HER DRESS was black and her coat, with its black fox collar, but at night no one would know the fox was real. Her hat didn't look as if it were a creation. Not at night, not with her pale horn-rimmed glasses; no one would look twice at a girl with glasses over her face.

Fifth Avenue was lighted, not with neon as Broadway, but it wasn't dark. Off the crosstown bus at Fiftieth, past the Cathedral, dark, yes, but there were people walking towards her and away from her, a young couple, students returning from a Carnegie concert, a goodly dressed man with heavy English brogans striding past her. And the windows beyond were light, the cosmetician's with the white down pussy cats pretending to grow on real pussy willow branches, the window of hand-created silver, the silver-etched imported china—bright candles on a bright street.

Only five blocks to Fifty-fifth, only a half block down with a great hotel on the corner and chipmunk taxi drivers waiting for the carriage trade. Her key ring was tight in her black gloved hand, her black antelope purse tight under her arm.

No reason to feel nervous at night, not even at eleven-thirty at night, in the heart of New York. Nothing ever happened to her kind of people; things happened to people living down those cross streets in old red bricks or old brownstones. Things threatened silver and gold dancers there in the Iridium Room across. But things didn't happen to her or anyone she knew.

Five short blocks and the sound of her black heels striking the walks. There were other sounds but she didn't hear anything but the heels. The other walkers didn't seem to notice that hers were too loud. She crossed Fifty-fifth, turned down her side of the street.

One delighted voice said, "Griselda! Fancy seeing you!"

The other one was laughing. "We thought you'd never come!"

She could see the tall silk hats, the shining white scarves, the dark coats, the sticks under their arms. Even in shadow she knew she had never seen the faces.

She was pleasant although wary. "I'm afraid you've made a mistake." Princeton boys or Yale, with a bit too much. But one had called her by name, by her own name.

One of them laughed. "Why, Griselda, how you talk!"

The other said, "And you so late for your appointment!"

"And we so patient."

They were moving her down the street as soldiers moved a condemned man. There wasn't a policeman. There never was at night in this neighborhood, by day yes, riding his fine horse, keeping traffic moving, but not at night. And Con was thousands of miles away.

She spoke insistently, "There's some mistake. You know there is. You've never seen me before."

They laughed uproariously. They had nice laughs, college boy laughs. She almost laughed with them, they were so merry. But each had a hand, ever so softly, under her elbow and she couldn't stop walking. They were moving her, even while they laughed, down the street to the two half-lighted windows, in one a swath of printed silk, in one two antique vases and an ostrich plume. If you turned between the shop windows, you went down a slightest incline to the door. It was locked at six. You opened it with your latch key, stepped into a small parquet vestibule; you rang for the elevator and waited. It was a self-running elevator, like in hospitals and old French pensions. Maybe that was why she was nervous, hearing her heels noisy on Fifth Avenue at night. She didn't like the feel of being shut in that elevator. But nothing happened to her kind. You pushed the four button and the car stopped at four. And then you were safe in Con's apartment, looking out of the windows, down at the cabs below, looking across the street where tall silk hats and furs came out of a great hotel.

She could say to these two, "Listen to me! A joke is a joke, boys, but you know that you don't know me and I don't know you and I want to go home now. If you don't stop this nonsense I'll speak to one of the drivers."

Suppose they didn't stop it? She could even speak to the taxi drivers. And suppose they just laughed too, or ignored her, thought she was crazy? She knew what she would do, walk past that entry way, pretend she lived farther on. Cross Madison, on the corner another hotel and a brightly lighted cocktail bar. She'd go in there and speak to someone. She didn't want to speak to the taxi drivers.

They were at the entrance to Con's. She moved her feet straight ahead, kept her eyes straight ahead, but two gloved hands gently on her two elbows veered her to the door.

She said, "You're making a mistake. I don't live here."

They laughed softly and the one on her left said, "You wouldn't fool us, would you, Griselda?" while the other opened her hand

and took away her keys. He had the door open and held it for her. She didn't know what to do. She could run. She could scream. But she couldn't do either. She was afraid. It was a dream and whatever she did there would be one on either side of her making her turn their way. But this couldn't be real. She'd never seen either of them before.

If she could reach the bells and push Gig's. He might be at home although he wasn't usually in this early. But one stood between her and the bells.

She was almost tearful with helpless rage. "I don't know why you're acting this way. You don't know me. You know you don't."

Hands walked her inside. Others closed the door. They were on either side of her again and one rang for the elevator. She could hear it creaking its way down the shaft.

One said to the other, "I don't think Griselda likes us."

The other put out his lower lip. "I don't know why. We like us."

They had such nice faces, as much as she could see of them, with the hats tilted over their eyes, the scarves high to their chins.

One held the elevator door. The other said, "You first, Griselda," but his hand was still soft on her arm white she stepped in. They followed, closed the door. One pushed button four.

She was cold now. "I don't know what this is all about. I don't know how you found out my name or where I'm staying. But I do think you're carrying a joke too far."

She had a fleeting suspicion that perhaps this was Con's idea of sport, or Gig's. But not Gig. He was too serious. Whatever it was she didn't like it. The elevator stopped. One was out; one behind her. One opened the door of her apartment, Con's apartment. They were inside, the door closed, the lights on. She stood in the middle of the floor watching them remove their tall hats, their white kid gloves, their white silk scarves, black formal over-coats; watching them lay down their sticks with the old-fashioned gold knobs topping them; watching them until they stood there, between her and the door, fashion plates in tails, white ties, opera pumps.

And only then was she really afraid, and for such a fantastic reason. Because one had honey-colored hair, sleek to his head, and one had bat-black hair; one had very blue eyes and one very black; one had the golden tan coloring of blonds and one the olive tan coloring of brunettes. But outside of that they looked exactly alike, unbelievably, frighteningly, alike. It was as if an artist had taken the same photograph and colored one dark, one fair. They were identical twins. And she was afraid.

The dark one was lighting a cigarette. The light one pulled up a comfortable cushioned chair. It was between her and the door. The dark one said, "Con won't mind if we have a drink. Will you join us, Griselda?"

She didn't answer but her fear ebbed. They did know Con. And they knew the apartment because the dark one opened the door into the tiny cupboard kitchen and she could hear bottles and glasses. She took off her coat then, standing there in the middle of the floor, and her glasses. They were such handsome men and she'd forgotten about wearing glasses. She put these on the mantel. The blond one took her coat and he opened the enormous closet of the living room, hung it on a hanger. She couldn't get to the entrance without passing him and even if she did it took two hands to turn that special bolt and open the door. She wasn't frightened now anyway. It was one of Con's jokes, something he considered funny.

The twin in the kitchen called out, "Bourbon or Scotch, Danny?" and the blond one came away from the closet.

"Bourbon, if it's good. Otherwise no. And what will you have, Griselda?"

She put her bag and gloves and hat on the table and sat on the couch. Danny sat beside her. She said, "I'll have a glass of sherry." He passed her a cigarette from the box on the table but for himself took one from a case out of his pocket. His cigarette was a French one with a small gold D engraved on the tip. The letter really was engraved. She knew without feeling it.

He called back, "Griselda will join us with a glass of sherry, David."

He was the best-looking man she'd ever seen until David came in with the drinks and then he was. They both were. David sat in the easy chair that Danny had placed. Danny remained beside her on the couch. But she wasn't afraid now. She sipped the sherry.

She spoke lightly, "Won't you tell me now what this is all about?"

David drank. "Not bad Scotch. How's the Bourbon, Danny?"

"Not bad at all."

"Did Con plan this? And why? Tell me about it." She was eager now to know. "I was frightened at first when you spoke to me and came in here. Who are you?"

They laughed again, those joyous laughs of theirs, and she laughed too, and then she stopped with something like a shiver. She didn't know why. Maybe because David was looking into his glass and his face wasn't laughing. Only his throat was. Maybe because she couldn't see into Danny's blue eyes. They were like jewels, not real.

He said, "Still pretending you don't know us, Griselda?"

She put her wineglass down and she sat very straight and stiff. "I don't know you." It seemed as if she'd been saying those words for hours. "I've never seen you before. I don't know who you are. You don't know me." She was a little hysterical. "Are you friends of Con's? You must be. Are you? What are you doing here?"

David pretended to sigh. "You aren't very hospitable, Griselda."

She was near to tears again but she buffeted them. "If you don't tell me right away what this is all about, I'll call the police."

Danny said, not too quickly, but easily, "I don't think you'd do that, Griselda."

David spread his thin hands, steel hands, you could tell. "What would you tell the police? Two young men escort you home, enter your apartment with you, the door opened by your own key, join you in a quiet drink. You couldn't say we were housebreakers nor disturbers of the peace. You could say we attacked you, I presume, but you'd have to tear yourself up a bit first. We wouldn't lay hands on you. And even then—"

She knew she was beaten. They wouldn't permit her to call the police anyway. She said, "You win. I'll be good. What do you want?"

David said, "We've just come to get our marbles."

Danny said, "That's all. Then we'll finish our drinks and leave you."

Then David looked at her and she was frightened again. His eyes, too, were jewels, not real, oblong black stones. You couldn't see into them nor beneath them. He smiled.

"We want our marbles. In particular one marble, a very blue one."

Danny was pleasant "We don't care about the others. Just give us our very blue marble and we'll go."

She held to her nerves. Maybe it was a dream, or maybe she was shut up in a crazy place. She wouldn't let go, scream and laugh and cry the way she wanted to. She tried to be natural, to be matter-of-fact. She couldn't help laughing a little.

"I haven't your marbles. There aren't any marbles here. You can look."

They didn't say anything.

She said, "I'll buy you some tomorrow when the stores open. I'll send you some if you wish me too. I'm sorry I haven't any for you now."

The dark David had stood up and he walked over to her until he was right in front of her. She was so frightened, for no reason, that she was shaking. He said, "We only want one marble, Griselda. The very blue one."

She screamed then. She didn't know why. Something about his eyes that were so dark, so opaque. Three things happened at once. She screamed. Danny's thumb and forefinger caught her wrist not softly now, but as if they were pincers. And someone pounded on her door. Three more things happened. She stopped her scream, Danny's fingers were on her knee, and there was a call, "Griselda, are you home?"

David spoke softly, "You answer it Griselda."

She was afraid to walk to that door, her back to the twins, but she did. She didn't hurry but she wanted to.

And outside was Gig, not six feet tall, not black handsome, nor golden handsome, not in evening attire. Just Gig, hardly taller than she, nondescript hair not combed very well, round spectacles over his round gray eyes, his old tweed working jacket over his pajamas, a book in his hand. She almost flung her arms around him. Gig, nice, sane Gig.

He said, "I didn't know you had company. I heard you come in and I'd just found that passage—"

She spoke rapidly, shrilly, on top of his words. "Come in. I'm not at all busy." She clung to his arm, pulled him inside. When she turned, the twins had their sticks under their arms, their hats on their heads.

Danny said, "We're just leaving."

David said, "It's been fun seeing you, Griselda."

They had their coats, their scarves, their gloves as they spoke.

She sidled Gig and herself past the door, leaving it wide for them.

Danny echoed, "Great fun, Griselda. See you soon."

"See you soon," David agreed.

They closed the door behind them. She heard them open the heavy elevator door; it was waiting, no one had used it since they had come up. She heard the whine of the machinery taking the cage downward. Only then did she release Gig's arm. She plopped down on the floor and began to laugh and cry, to cry and laugh.

2

Gig said, "Stop it! Stop it, Griselda!" He looked so utterly bewildered, woebegone, she laughed harder, cried harder. But she choked out, "Bolt that door. Lock and bolt that door."

He told her, "It is bolted. It bolts itself, Griselda. Are you crazy?"

She hugged her knees. "I think I am. Somebody's crazy. Or

everybody's crazy." She couldn't stop the awful noises she was making.

He said, "You've got to stop it. You'll make yourself sick." Then he had an idea. He went into the kitchen and poured out half a tumbler of Scotch. He knelt down and pushed it op to her mouth. She drank it. It made her choke but it quieted her.

He helped her up from the floor to the couch. "Now can you tell me? What's happened?"

She said she didn't know. She began, "Does Con play mar— mar—mar—" Then she started laughing again but she stopped herself. She couldn't say it without laughing. It was too ridiculous. Leggy Con, on the floor shooting marbles.

Gig was troubled. He begged, "Try and tell me, Griselda." He was so sane. "Or don't if you'd rather not."

She caught his hand. "I want to tell you. Let me have a cigarette first. Then maybe I can make sense."

He found the box, as usual he had only a smelly pipe in his pockets, and lit her cigarette.

She leaned against the pillows. "I'll tell you. I've been nervous ever since I came, Gig, all this past week. I don't know why. Every night I've been sort of—well,—frightened—coming home from the theater, or from Ann's. Whenever I've been out alone, I've been—well, just plain scared."

She didn't expect him to understand. He didn't. He blinked behind his spectacles. He wasn't an imaginator.

She explained, "Not really scared, Gig. Just uneasy." She twisted on the couch until she could see his face. "Do you suppose something inside of us has premonitions—warns us to be careful? And yet if anyone had definitely told me, I'd have laughed. I'd have told them what I told myself. Things don't happen to people like us."

He was packing his pipe. "Well, they don't happen to people like me. But I'd say from what Con has told me that quite a lot has happened to you in your twenty-four years."

"Oh, that. I don't mean that." She was impatient. "I mean things like—horrible things—" She shivered a little.

He was startled. "Was tonight horrible?"

She could tell it now, although it didn't sound horrible, nor even as insane as it had been in happening. She told of the corner meeting, the entrance, all but the marbles. She couldn't speak of that yet.

He asked, puzzled. "They called you by name? And you didn't know them?"

"I've never seen them before in all my life. It might have been a joke. Do you think—did Con know them? Have you seen them before?"

He hadn't. "Of course I don't know about Con. He has multitudes of friends. I don't know many of them by sight or otherwise. Living across the hall as we do we still don't see much of each other. You know New York. That's why I was surprised to see you. I didn't even know you were coming East."

She said, "I know," but she wasn't thinking about Gig's surprised face when he came out of his apartment and saw her, surrounded by bags, opening the door of Con's apartment. She was thinking of marbles, of the ludicrousness of Con and marbles.

He asked, "You don't know who these men are?"

It wasn't a question but she answered, "They called each other David and Danny." She repeated, "David—Danny."

He was thoughtful. "There's Dave Cling—used to be on the *Times* with Con, but it wasn't he." And then he asked, all at sea, "But what did they want?"

She could tell him now, speak the insane words soberly, "They wanted their marbles."

Gig's mild eyes blinked.

"Particularly a very blue marble." She let him take it in before asking, "Does that mean anything to you?"

He repeated, "Their marbles—a very blue marble."

She asked, "Did Con ever play marbles?"

"My God, no!" He said, "I've never heard anything like it. Marbles—blue marbles—"

"One blue marble," she corrected.

He was thoughtful, "Do you think they were crazy?"

She nodded. "Part of the time I thought so, but"—she had to admit it—"they were saner than I was."

"Were they—" he didn't know how to phrase it—"did they offer any violence to you?"

She said they didn't, then she remembered tight fingers on her wrist, but she didn't correct herself.

He wondered, sucking at his pipe, if they should notify the police. She shook her head. "There's nothing to notify about that I can see. They didn't do anything. Besides I don't know who they are." She yawned. That tumbler was beginning to have effect.

He asked, "I don't suppose you've seen anything of any marbles around here—or one blue marble?"

She yawned again. "Of course not, Gig. I haven't gone through Con's boxes in there, nor the drawers he left filled. But I don't think I'd find marbles if I did."

"I don't imagine that you would," he agreed. "It is strange. It's the strangest thing I've ever heard of. What can we do? What can I do?"

She stood on her feet, a little dizzy from the dose. She said, "You can stay here tonight."

"I couldn't do that!"

She was firm. "You'll have to. Or let me stay with you. I won't be alone, Gig. I'm afraid."

He twittered, "I couldn't stay all night with you, Griselda."

"You must. I wouldn't dare be alone."

He didn't believe the men would return, but he didn't speak with much sincerity.

She told him, "You heard what they said."

He had heard. But he didn't think they'd return tonight.

She was serious, yawning again. "It would be like them to come back tonight. They are—" She couldn't find the word.

He supplied, "Erratic."

"Yes. Crazy." She started to the bedroom but her toes stopped on the edge of the rug. "You don't mind looking in there first, Gig?"

He stammered, "N-no. Of course I don't." He was a professor and not very tall but his shoulders were brawny.

Only two rooms at Con's, an old apartment building in the middle of the city. Shops on the street floor and the first floor. Only four floors of apartments, two to the floor, and the small single above where the superintendent lived. Fourth floor was safe, Con's on the front, Gig's on the back. Two rooms at Con's, the great high-ceilinged living room with the wood-burning fireplace, the extra large closet, the cupboard kitchen; bedroom with the same high ceiling, the like fireplace, a smaller closet, and a great bathroom. No way to get into the bathroom but the bedroom door and a small skylight window opening into a shaft. But in the bedroom a door leading to the backstairs which you must use if the elevator was out of order or stuck. Con had warned of the peculiarities of the elevator but it hadn't gone wrong in her week of residence. Double bolts on the door to the backstairs. Each night she had peered at those bolts, making certain they were caught. But she hadn't touched them; she was afraid something might be standing outside. She heard Gig there now opening those bolts and the door. She shivered. She heard him close and bolt again.

When he returned he said, "It's perfectly safe. I even looked in the shower curtain and under the bed." No one could get under that low-set modern bed. He felt the stem of his pipe. "But if you're afraid I will stay here on the couch."

She said, "No, you won't. You'll stay in the bedroom. I'll sleep in a chair and you take the bed. Or if you insist I'll help you move the couch in there. But I won't stay alone." She touched his sleeve. "I'm not afraid of you, Gig. I'm afraid of them."

He didn't look at her. "Whatever you say, Griselda." He began picking up the empty glasses and taking them to the kitchen. She went in the bedroom but she didn't close the door between. For his sake she undressed in the bathroom, put on her white satin pajamas and her white tweed man-like dressing gown. She turned down the bed and called to him.

He came in. He said, "I suppose I shouldn't have washed the tumblers."

She shook her head. "Of course not. Bette comes at nine."

"I mean fingerprints."

Her mouth made an O. "I didn't think. But it wouldn't do any good." She took two extra blankets from the old cherrywood cabinet. "There's no reason for either of us to sleep in the chair. The bed's enormous. I'll sleep inside and you out." She felt mid-Victorian, but he was such a mouse. She spoke coaxingly, "You'll be more comfortable than in a chair and you have to teach tomorrow."

He was like a little boy. "All right, Griselda." He took off his spectacles and laid them on the left bed table.

She put her white coat on the foot of the bed and edged into the right-hand place. He lay far at the left and pulled the blankets over him. He didn't remove his coat.

She asked, "Do you think it would hurt to leave one lamp on?"

He didn't complain but he did say, "I can't sleep with a light on."

He had been too helpful. She turned out the lamp. It was like being in bed alone, but she could hear breathing. She felt safe. Then she asked, "What did you mean—plenty of things happen to me?"

He was apologetic. "It seems as if they do. Going to California four years ago to visit your aunt, like any popular society girl, and having the movies insist on starring you. Being really a great star when barely out of your teens—then leaving pictures entirely in one year despite all the offers they made. And now starting out again as a designer—" He broke off, "Con told me this."

She yawned. "Uh-huh. But that isn't really having things happen. I just photograph."

He said professorially, "Acting takes more than photography. Although you have beauty."

She didn't answer. People thought she had beauty. She didn't. Regular features were to be expected in ordinary people, and gray eyes were nothing. Hers looked big and bright because she needed glasses. Without glasses the straining widened the pupils. Her only real beauty was her hair, freak hair, naturally golden. It had retained unaided the gold of a child's hair, of a princess. She liked the way she wore it now, like a wig it was, turned below her ears, smoothed away from her forehead. Her skin and figure were good but that too was ordinary, to be expected when one swam and danced and rode and didn't gorge on sugars. Nothing sensational about her. She had hated being in the pictures even that one year, being fussed over.

He wondered, "Perhaps they had seen you in pictures."

She said sleepily, "But they called me by my own name, Griselda—not Mariel York. And I've been off the screen three years."

He spoke as sleepily, "That's right."

She was almost sliding into deep sleep when he spoke again. "I really don't like staying here. Con is my friend."

She broke in rudely, "Don't be ridiculous. You know Con and I have been divorced for four years."

Continued in
The So Blue Marble...

14
MYS